Abraham Lincoln

The Great Emancipator

Illustrated by Jerry Robinson

Abraham Lincoln

The Great Emancipator

by Augusta Stevenson

Aladdin Paperbacks

First Aladdin Paperbacks edition 1986
Copyright © 1932, 1953, 1959 by the Bobbs-Merrill Company, Inc.

ALADDIN PAPERBACKS
An imprint of Simon & Schuster Children's Publishing Division
1230 Avenue of the Americas, New York, NY 10020

Manufactured in the United States of America

38 40 39

Library of Congress Cataloging-in-Publication Data
Stevenson, Augusta.
Abraham Lincoln, the Great Emancipator.
Reprint of the ed.: Indianapolis : Bobbs-Merrill, 1982, c1959.
Published 1932 under title: Abe Lincoln, frontier boy.
p.   cm. — (Childhood of Famous Americans)
Summary: Recounts the childhood of the man who was President during the Civil War.
1. Lincoln, Abraham, 1809–1865—Childhood and youth—Juvenile literature.
2. Presidents—United States—Biography—Juvenile literature.
[1. Lincoln, Abraham, 1809–1865.   2. Presidents.]
I. Robinson, Jerry, ill.   II. Title.
[E457.905.S72   1986]   973.7'092'4   [B] [92]   86-10732
ISBN-13: 978-0-02-042030-9 (Aladdin pbk.)
ISBN-10: 0-02-042030-7 (Aladdin pbk.)

*With appreciation to
Jessica Brown Mannon*

Illustrations

Full pages

Numerous smaller illustrations

Contents

Books by Augusta Stevenson

Abraham Lincoln

The Great Emancipator

Abe's First Toy

THERE WAS once a little boy who lived in a little cabin on a little farm in a little clearing on a little creek. Now this little creek had a little name— *Knob*. But the boy had a big name—*Abraham*.

Little Knob Creek was in the great big state of Kentucky. Abraham was born February 12, 1809, on another farm about ten miles away. This farm was not on Knob Creek, but it was in the great big state of Kentucky.

Little Abraham was in the great big family of Lincolns. There were his father and mother and older sister, Sarah. He lived with them, of course. Then there were many aunts and uncles.

There were more cousins than he could count. He didn't see any of these relatives very often, because they lived too far away.

Nobody in the Lincoln family called Abraham by his big name. "Abraham is too long," everyone agreed. "Abe is better."

So Abe he was, to his family and his friends. The name stayed with him, even when he became a man and as long as he lived.

Abe liked his home on Knob Creek. But sometimes he wished that the Lincoln farm was not so far from other farms. The nearest neighbors lived miles away in other clearings in the forest. They lived too far away for him to play with any of their children.

Sarah played with Abe when she had time, but she liked to play with dolls. Abe couldn't help wishing that he had a brother or some other boy to play with. A boy would like to do the things that he liked to do.

One morning Abe and Sarah were playing out-doors. Before long Sarah ran into the cabin, cry-ing. "Oh, Mother!" she said. "Abe won't play with me."

Mrs. Lincoln was surprised. "What is the matter?" she asked. "Have you children been quarreling?"

"No, Mother, we didn't quarrel, but Abe wouldn't play with my doll. It's a new doll, too, and it's made from the largest corncob Father could find."

"That's true," said Mr. Lincoln. "It was the largest one in the field."

"It is a fine doll, Sarah," said Mother. "Why doesn't Abe like it?"

"I don't know," said Sarah. "He said he wouldn't play girl games any more."

"Well! Well!" said Mother. "I am surprised to hear that Abe won't play with a doll."

"Ha! ha!" laughed Father. "Abe is growing up, Nancy."

"But he is only five and a half, Thomas."

"He is growing up just the same. You must play something else with Abe, Sarah."

"There isn't anything else to play, Father."

"If they only had some toys they could play better," said Mother.

"I suppose they could," said Father, "but toys cost money and I haven't finished paying for this farm."

"Abe wants a little wagon," said Sarah.

"Couldn't you make one, Thomas?" asked Mrs. Lincoln. "You are such a good carpenter. You made our wooden plates."

"Of course I could make a little wagon," said Mr. Lincoln, "but I won't have time this summer. Maybe I can next winter."

"But Abe needs something to play with now," said Mother. "He is so lonesome. Sarah helps

14

me with the work and that leaves Abe alone so much. No little boys to play with. No one but just himself."

"I tell you what I'll do," said Father. "I'm going to Thomas Hall's sale this morning to buy some tools, and if I can find a toy wagon I'll buy it. That is, if it doesn't cost too much."

"Oh, of course," said Mother, "if it doesn't cost too much."

THE SALE

The Halls were going to move away. Almost everything they owned was for sale, and people came from miles around to buy.

Mr. Lincoln met neighbors from up the creek and down the creek and over the hills.

They were all glad to see him. They liked him, and, besides, he was the best judge of horses in that part of Kentucky.

15

"I've been waiting for you, Thomas," said a
man. "I want to buy a horse, but I want your
opinion first."

Mr. Lincoln examined the horse carefully and
told the man what it was worth.

Then other men asked him about horses and
kept him busy so long he forgot all about that
toy wagon for Abe.

At last he bought his tools and told his friends good-by.

As he went for his horse, two men passed him. They were carrying a long settee.

"I hope it will go in my wagon," said one.

"Wagon!" said Mr. Lincoln out loud. "Oh, yes! Wagon!" Then he hurried back to the cabin and began to look about.

On a table were dishes, forks, knives, spoons, buckets, pots and pans. On the floor were featherbeds, pillows, coverlets, quilts and skins. There seemed to be everything but toys.

"What are you looking for, Mr. Lincoln?" asked Mrs. Hall. "Perhaps I can help you."

"I want a little wagon for Abe, Mrs. Hall, but I don't see any toys."

Mrs. Hall laughed. "Look up there," she said.

She pointed to the shelf over the fireplace.

Mr. Lincoln looked up. Then he laughed, for there was a little toy wagon!

"I have ten cents I can spend," he said.

"It's yours," said Mrs. Hall. "See! It's marked eight cents."

"Good!" said Mr. Lincoln. He paid the money, took the wagon and started for the little log cabin on Knob Creek.

ABE WATCHES

Outside this cabin, on a stump, sat a little black-haired boy watching the road. He looked and he looked, but his father did not come.

His mother had said that Father would be home for supper, but supper was over and he hadn't come. Now the sun was going down behind the hill. Soon it would be dark.

"Abe!" called Mrs. Lincoln from the door. "It's too late for you to be outside."

"May I wait till Father comes?"

"No, Abe. It's too damp. You'll get chilled."

18

Abe went into the cabin at once.

"Why, Abe," said Sarah, "you're crying!"

"I want my wagon," said Abe.

Mother put her arms around the boy and spoke to him gently.

"Abe," she said, "Father wasn't sure he could find a wagon, was he?"

"No," said Abe.

"And he wasn't sure he would have enough money to buy it, was he?"

"No," said Abe.

"Then you shouldn't be crying when he comes home. It will make him feel bad."

"I won't cry any more," said Abe.

"That's fine," said Mother. "Sarah, Abe is a little man. Don't tell Father he cried."

"I won't," said Sarah. "But Father might lose the wagon on the way home."

"Lose it!" Abe said. "How could he lose it?"

"It might fall in the creek and he couldn't get

it out," said Sarah. "Or maybe he wouldn't even know it fell."

Abe's lips trembled. He looked as if he were going to cry again.

"Yes," said Mother, "all those things might happen."

She smiled at Abe, and Abe smiled back. Then he said bravely, "I won't cry anyway."

Just then the door opened, and in came Mr. Lincoln. "Here's your wagon, Abe!" he said.

"Oh!" said Abe. "Oh! Oh!"

That was all Abe could say.

Abe pulled the wagon over to the fireplace. He sat down on the floor and turned the wagon upside down. With his fingers he made the wheels go round and round. After a while he turned the wagon right side up again and began to pull it around the room.

"Will you give my doll a ride in your wagon, Abe?" Sarah asked.

Before Abe could answer, Mother said, "Wait until tomorrow, Sarah. Abe has waited so long for his wagon. Just let him do whatever he wants to with it tonight."

"Oh, I'd like to give the doll a ride," said Abe. "That's not like playing with one."

Back and forth Abe pulled the wagon. There wasn't a happier boy in the world that night than little Abe Lincoln.

School-butter

SARAH AND Abe were ready for their first day of school. They were so excited they scarcely knew what they were doing. Sarah had braided her two pigtails four times. Abe had combed his hair five times.

Sarah wore her new dress of linsey-woolsey that her mother had woven and made. She was barefooted and bareheaded. Her pigtails hung down her back.

Abe wore his new pants. They were linsey-woolsey like his shirt and had been woven and made by his mother. He wore a coonskin cap, but he was barefooted like Sarah.

Both children were as clean as soap and water could make them.

"Here are two corndodgers for your dinner," said Mother. "Put them in your pocket, Sarah. If you children want berries you can pick them at noon. There are plenty in the woods around the schoolhouse."

"May I carry your speller, Sarah?" asked Abe, as he reached for the book.

"I don't care," Sarah said.

Just then Mr. Lincoln came in. "Sarah," he said, "tell the schoolmaster that I will buy a speller for Abe soon—the next time I go to a sale. He can study with you for a week or so."

"Don't I need a reader, too?" asked Sarah.

"Not until you have finished your speller," said Mother.

"Be sure to study it out loud," said Father. "The teacher won't know you are studying if you don't."

"All right," said Sarah, "I will."

"I will, too," said Abe.

"It's time for you children to start now," said Mother. "You must not be late on the first day." She kissed them, and Father patted Abe's black head and Sarah's brown one.

The children followed the path across the clearing and into the woods. Soon they were out of sight.

Mrs. Lincoln wiped the tears from her eyes. "It's so far for them to walk," she said. "Three miles every day and the path is rough."

"It can't be helped, Nancy. They are lucky to go to school at all. There are several children around here who can't afford to go."

"We can't really afford to send the children ourselves," said Nancy.

"I'll do extra work this winter," said Thomas, "carpenter work. I think I'll make enough to pay the schoolmaster."

"I hope you will," Nancy said. "I'm so anxious for the children to learn."

"Yes," said Thomas, "they should learn to read and write."

AFTER SCHOOL

Late that afternoon Sarah came home from school alone.

"Mother! Father!" she cried as she hurried into the cabin. "Abe's gone!"

"Gone!" said Father. "Gone where?"

"I don't know," said Sarah. Then she began to cry.

"Come, come, dear, don't cry," Mother said. "Sit here by me on the bench. Now, then, tell us what happened."

"Just as school was out," said Sarah, "we heard some boys outside calling names at us."

"At you and Abe?" Mother asked.

26

"No," said Sarah, "at all of us. I couldn't understand what they said, but it made the schoolboys mad."

"Was it 'School-butter'?" asked Father.

"Yes, that was it! Then they ran, and our boys ran after them, and Abe went, too."

"Abe went!" cried Mother, alarmed.

"I told him not to, but the boys called him. I guess he thought he had to go."

Mrs. Lincoln was frightened. "The big boys will run ahead and leave him," she said. "He will get lost in the woods."

"I'll go after him," said Mr. Lincoln. "Don't worry, Nancy, I'll find him."

Then he ran out of the cabin. He didn't even stop to get his cap.

Sarah cried again. "I'm afraid Abe will fall in the creek," she said.

Mother was afraid of that, too, but she didn't want Sarah to know it. So she said, "Father will find him. Now then, do you know why those boys called 'School-butter'?"

"No, Mother, I don't."

"They wanted to make fun of the children who go to school."

"Why?" asked Sarah.

"I think they really want to go to school themselves, but their folks can't afford to send them. So they pretend it's silly to go, sort of soft—like butter."

"Oh, yes," said Sarah. "I understand."

"Now let's get a good supper for Father and Abe. I'll make some flour biscuits," said Mother.

"Flour biscuits!" Sarah cried. And her eyes nearly popped right out of her head.

"It will be a treat for all of us," said Mother. "Please put these apples in the hot ashes, Sarah. Then you may fill this gourd with maple sugar."

"Oh! Oh!" said Sarah. "Won't a good supper make Abe happy!"

Mr. Lincoln ran into the woods calling, "Abe! Abe!"

There was no answer, so he ran up the trail toward the schoolhouse. Sometimes he stumbled over large tree roots. Once he caught his foot in a wild grapevine and fell. But in an instant he was up and running again.

He kept on calling Abe, but there was only silence in the great forest.

At last he reached the clearing where the log schoolhouse stood. There wasn't a boy or a girl to be seen, so into the woods he went again. On and on up the trail he went.

"Abe!" he called again and again. "Abe! Abe! Abe!"

There was no answer and not even a glimpse of a little black-haired boy.

It began to get dark in the woods, but still Mr. Lincoln went on. At last he stopped.

"Abe! Abe! Where are you?" he called once more, but there was no answer.

"Abe couldn't have come any farther," he said to himself. "He couldn't walk any farther."

So he turned and went back on the trail toward the schoolhouse. He hoped the schoolmaster would still be there. The two of them could go together to hunt for Abe. They would stop at every cabin along the creek, and every neighbor would join them. They would all take torches and look in the creek.

Mr. Lincoln came to the clearing and went in the schoolhouse. There sat the master at his desk, writing.

"Mr. Riney!" said Mr. Lincoln. "I'm hunting Abe. He's lost!"

"Look there," said Mr. Riney. He pointed to a bench.

Mr. Lincoln looked. Abe was lying on it, sound asleep!

"He ran after the boys," said Mr. Riney, "and I ran after him and brought him back. I was just getting ready to take him home."

"I'm much obliged to you, Mr. Riney," said Mr. Lincoln. "I was afraid he might have fallen into the creek and been drowned." Then he went to the bench and tried to awaken Abe.

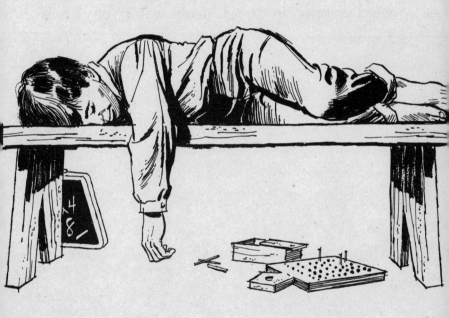

First he shook him gently by the shoulder.

"Abe! Abe!" he said. "Wake up!"

Abe opened his eyes, but he was still half asleep.

"School-butter!" shouted the master.

Then Abe awoke and jumped up.

The men laughed. Abe laughed. Then Mr. Lincoln took Mr. Riney and Abe to a very, very good supper in the Lincoln cabin on Knob Creek.

Grandfather and the Indians

ONE RAINY day Mother Nancy Lincoln was spinning wool.

Sarah and Abe were watching her. They loved to watch Mother spin. They loved to watch that great wheel go round and round. They loved to see the spindle turn.

"Mother," said Abe, "I would rather watch you spin than do anything else."

"So would I," said Sarah.

Mrs. Lincoln laughed. "I know something that both of you would rather do," she said. "You would much rather listen to your father tell some of his stories."

Sarah and Abe didn't know what to say. They did love to hear Father tell stories.

Mother laughed again. "That's all right, children," she said. "There isn't anyone who can tell stories as well as your father. The neighbors all say that, and you know they visit us sometimes just to hear him."

"I know they do," said Sarah proudly.

"I'm going to tell stories, too, when I'm a man," said Abe.

Just then the door was opened quickly, and in came Father Thomas Lincoln with a gust of wind and rain. He was dripping wet—his clothes, his coonskin cap, his deerskin moccasins.

"This is a bad storm," he said. "I can't work in the field, and I can't work in the woods. I can't even hunt or fish."

"It will give you a chance to rest," said Mrs. Lincoln. "Sarah, take your father's wet cap. Abe, take his moccasins."

Sarah hung the dripping cap on a peg in the wall across the room from the fireplace. Abe put the dripping moccasins in a corner that was not too near the fireplace.

Mr. Lincoln was pleased. "I see you children know how to take care of skins as well as little Indians do," he said.

He sat on the fireside bench and soon his wet clothes began to dry.

"Would you like to hear a story, children?" he asked.

"Yes! Yes!" cried Sarah and Abe.

"Bring up your stools and I'll tell you a true story. It's about your Grandfather Abraham Lincoln."

"That's my name, too," said Abe.

"You were named for him," said Mr. Lincoln, "and I hope you will grow up to be as brave a man as he was."

"Wasn't he afraid of anything?" Abe asked.

"Nothing," said Father, "not even Indians. He was a soldier in the Indian War."

"Did he wear a blue coat with brass buttons?" asked Sarah.

"Indeed he did," Father said. "He was the captain of his company, and he helped to drive the Indians out of these woods."

"Never forget that, children," said Mother, "and always be good to soldiers."

"What could I do for a soldier?" Abe asked.

"You could show respect by taking off your cap when you meet one," said Father.

"You could get him a drink of water," said Mother, "and give him some food."

"What do soldiers eat?" Sarah asked.

"Anything they can get," said Father, "and plenty of that."

Mother laughed. The children laughed. Then Father said, "Abe, throw a log on the fire, and I'll tell you the story."

FATHER'S STORY

Now Abe was only seven years old, but he lifted a log and put it in the fireplace.

"Isn't Abe strong!" said Sarah.

"I like to be strong," Abe said. "I can help Father in the field."

Father nodded. "Just as I helped my father when I was a little boy. In fact, that is part of my story. You see, children, my father was a farmer, just as I am. Only he owned more land and horses and cows than I do."

"We own horses," said Abe.

"We own cows," said Sarah, "and calves."

"Not half as many as my father had," said Mr. Lincoln, "and he owned more than two thousand acres of land."

"He must have been rich," said Sarah.

"No, Sarah, he wasn't rich. He worked in his fields every day, and my brothers and I worked with him. One spring morning when I was about six years old, he took me to a cornfield that was close to the woods."

"Were there Indians in the woods?" asked Abe.

"There had been, but Father thought they would never return. The soldiers had built a fort near our farm, so we felt quite safe.

"Father stood there and looked over the field. 'Too many weeds,' he said. 'We'll pull them, Thomas.' He stooped over, but he didn't pull a single weed. Something terrible happened!"

38

"What? What?" cried Sarah and Abe.

"I heard a shot. I saw my father fall. He didn't speak again. He was dead."

"Indians!" said Abe.

"Indians!" said Sarah.

"Yes," said Father, "Indians. They were hiding in the woods, waiting for Father to come to the cornfield."

"Poor Grandfather," said Sarah.

"They killed one of the best men in the country," said Mr. Lincoln. "And that wasn't all, children. They tried to get me."

"You!" cried the children.

"An Indian ran out of the woods and seized me. He began to drag me out of the field."

"Oh! Oh!" cried Sarah and Abe.

"I was frightened nearly to death. I thought I would never see my mother again."

"Poor little boy," said Mrs. Lincoln.

"We were now at the edge of the field. An-

other step or two and the Indian would have me in the woods. But again something happened! I heard another shot and I saw the Indian fall. He didn't speak or move. He was dead."

"Who shot him?" asked Abe.

"My oldest brother, and he was only twelve. He shot from our cabin door."

"But he might have hit you instead of the Indian!" said Abe. "The Indian had hold of you when your brother fired."

"He had to take the chance," said Mr. Lincoln. "My second brother had run to the fort for the soldiers. My mother could see other Indians in the woods, and she was afraid I wouldn't reach the cabin alive.

"By that time the soldiers had come. They drove the Indians out of the woods and they never returned."

"I'm sorry about Grandfather," said Abe, "but I'm glad that Indian didn't get you."

Sarah and Abe Go Fishing

"MOTHER," asked Abe, "do you need any more wood?"

"No, Abe," said Mrs. Lincoln, "you have brought all I need today."

"Do you need any more water?"

Mrs. Lincoln looked at the water buckets. "Why, they are full!" she said. "You must have worked pretty fast, Abe."

"I'd like to go fishing, Mother."

"You have earned it, my dear boy. You may go and you may stay all afternoon."

"I want to go, too," said Sarah.

"No," said Mother, "you aren't old enough."

"I'm older than Abe," said Sarah. "I'm two years older."

"But Abe is larger and stronger, and he knows how to take care of himself."

"I'll take care of her," said Abe. "I won't let her go near the deep water."

"Very well, then. Go along, children."

The children ran all the way to the creek. They had no fishing poles or lines or hooks, but they knew just what to do. They found a place where the creek was shallow. They stooped over and held their hands in the water.

"Don't let them slip through your hands," said Abe. "Fish are slippery."

Then they waited and waited and waited. Their arms ached and their necks and backs ached, but still they stooped and waited.

"Let's go home," Sarah said at last.

"Not yet," said Abe. "You can play on the bank, Sarah."

And Abe went on fishing.

Sarah found some acorns under a great oak tree. So for a long time she was very busy.

She made acorn cups and saucers. She made an acorn sugar bowl and cream pitcher. She made acorn bowls for berries and mush.

Then she played she was drinking sassafras tea from the cups. She used play cream and play sugar. She ate a bowl of play mush and a bowl of play berries.

Now she was tired of playing. "Abe!" she called. "Let's go home!"

"Not yet," said Abe. "Wait."

And Abe went on fishing.

Sarah looked about for something else to do. Her keen eyes found some wild grapes high on a large vine. The vine grew close by a giant tree and had fastened itself around it. It was almost as strong as the tree and as large around as Abe's arm.

So up that vine went Sarah, just like a little squirrel. Then she sat in a crook of the vine and ate grapes until she couldn't eat another one.

"Come on, Abe!" she called at last. "Let's go home!"

"Not yet," said Abe. "Wait."

And Abe went on fishing.

Sarah swung herself to the ground. Near by was a mother robin feeding a young robin. Sarah thought it would be fun to count the worms it ate. So she sat on a log, leaned against a tree and began to count. "One, two, three, four, five, six, seven, eight, nine, ten———"

Sarah's dark eyes closed. Sarah's brown head nodded—Sarah was asleep.

And Abe went on fishing.

Sarah didn't know she went to sleep. She didn't know how long she slept. But she did know that someone was shaking her. She opened her eyes and there was Abe by her side.

"Look!" he said. "I've caught a fish!"

"It isn't very large," said Sarah.

"No, but it's a fish," said Abe, "and that's what I was fishing for."

"You were a long time," said Sarah.

"I don't care, I caught it," said Abe. "Now we'll go home."

46

Then Sarah and Abe started home. They went through the woods, between the great, great trees. As they walked along the narrow path, they talked and talked and talked.

They weren't talking about bears or wildcats or snakes.

No indeed! They didn't even think of bears, and they didn't think of wildcats or snakes.

They talked about Abe's fish. It was his first fish, and he had caught it with his hands. He was proud of that, and he had a right to be proud. Sarah had tried to catch a fish with her hands. She knew how hard it was.

"Isn't your back tired, Abe?" she asked. "You had to lean over the water so long."

"Yes," said Abe, "but I don't care. I was determined to catch a fish."

"Mother will be glad to have it. She will fry it for our supper."

47

Just then they heard a voice. Someone called, "Wait, children!"

The children turned. A strange man was coming toward them. He was smiling and waving his hand.

"I want to talk with you," he called. "I have been alone in this forest all day, and I'm lonesome."

Abe's gray eyes opened wide. The man wore a blue coat with brass buttons!

Abe's hat came off quickly.

"Oh!" he said. "You are a soldier!"

"Yes," said the man, "I'm a soldier. I've been out fighting Indians."

"Indians!" gasped Sarah. "Do you think they will come to our cabin?"

"You needn't be afraid," said the man. "They are far away from here."

"Can't I get you a drink of clear, cold water?" asked Abe.

"Thank you, but I found a spring on the hill and I drank enough for a week."

Then the soldier laughed, and Abe and Sarah laughed, too.

"Can't I get you something to eat?" asked Abe next.

"I wish you could," said the soldier. "I'm hungry."

"Can't you come home with us to supper?" Sarah asked. "Mother would be very glad to have you."

"So would Father," Abe said. "His father was a soldier, too."

"Thank you both, but I must go on. I'll try to get some supper where I camp for the night. I'll find some grapes or berries."

"Take my fish, sir. You could cook it for your supper."

"No, no, my boy! Why, that's the only fish you have!"

"Please take it, sir. I want to do something for you."

"Why?" the man asked.

"Because you are a soldier," Abe said.

"Bless your kind heart!" the man said. "Yes, I'll take your fish, and I'll fry it for my supper. And thanks to you, little boy, many thanks."

"I want to be kind to all soldiers," said Abe.

"I hope you will be," said the man, "always, as long as you live."

Forest Adventures

SOMETIMES Abe had a little boy to play with now. His name was Austin Gollaher, and he lived with his parents in a log cabin on Knob Creek.

The Gollaher cabin was three miles from the Lincoln cabin, and the road was very rough. It went up a steep hill, down a steep hill, over great roots and rocks and bumps.

So the two families couldn't visit very often. But whenever Mrs. Gollaher visited Mrs. Lincoln, she took Austin. And whenever Mrs. Lincoln visited Mrs. Gollaher, she took Abe.

Austin was two years older than Abe, but Abe

51

was now so large and strong that he could do everything Austin could.

The boys had great fun together. They played in the woods around their cabins. They played in the creek near their cabins. But deep into the forest, away from the trails, they were never allowed to go.

"You boys must wait until you learn more about the forest," said Mr. Lincoln. "It is full of danger."

"Yes, indeed," said Mr. Gollaher, "there is great danger to all who do not understand the forest's language."

"What do you mean?" asked Austin.

"How can a forest have a language?" Abe wanted to know.

"The forest has many sounds and warnings, and you must know what they mean," said Mr. Gollaher. "When you have learned that, you will know its language."

"And if you don't obey its warnings, you may never get out alive," added Mr. Lincoln.

The boys were obedient. Not once did they run away to play in the deep woods.

Several months passed. Then one day Mr. Lincoln said, "Boys, you are old enough now to study the forest. When do you want to begin your lessons?"

"Now, Father," said Abe, "if that suits you."

"Yes," said Austin, "now, Mr. Lincoln, if you please."

First, Mr. Lincoln taught them to walk like Indians, without making a noise. They learned to keep away from dry leaves and broken twigs. They learned to pass bushes without breaking off a leaf. They learned to cover their tracks and to follow the tracks of others.

Mr. Lincoln showed them how to hide and how to crawl so quietly that one could scarcely see the grass move.

All this was not learned in one day. The boys practiced weeks and weeks.

At last Mr. Lincoln was satisfied.

"You boys do very well," he said, "as well as Indian boys of your age."

LISTENING LESSONS

Then Mr. Lincoln taught the boys to listen to the sounds of the forest. "You must know all the cries and sounds of birds and beasts," he said. "You must know what they mean."

He taught them the cries of the eagle and panther, the hiss of the snake and its rattle, the scream of the wildcat and the different growls of the bear.

It took a long, long time to learn these sounds. It was as hard as arithmetic, but the two boys kept at it, and after a while their ears were as sharp as razors.

When a wild bird called they could answer. They could hoot almost as well as a screech owl.

But when they heard the cry of an eagle, they knew they had to hide. And when they heard a rattle, they ran straight home.

TRACKING LESSONS

From Mr. Gollaher the boys learned the tracks of animals, birds and snakes. This took a long time, too. But the boys kept at it, and after a while their eyes were as sharp as their ears.

They followed a fox's track to his den and saw the handsome fellow.

They followed a rabbit's tracks to her nest and saw the baby rabbits.

They followed deer tracks to a pool and saw the pretty deer drinking.

They followed the tracks of a ground hog and saw him digging his home.

They followed the tracks of a beaver and saw him cutting a tree.

Some tracks they did not follow.

"Boys," said Mr. Gollaher, "when you see bear tracks, you must go the other way. And you must never follow the tracks of panthers or wildcats."

The boys obeyed him. They knew now that it was "Safety First" in the forest.

They learned to notice everything. If a twig was broken they saw it. If the moss was crushed they knew it.

One day they thought they saw a log move. Neither boy thought of running to the log and jumping on it. Neither boy screamed.

No, indeed! They hid behind a tree and watched. Not one word did they speak. Not one sound did they make.

The log moved again, and then something came out of it—a big, black bear!

The two boys ran home, and they ran just as fast as their legs could carry them.

THE CRY IN THE WOODS

One summer day Abe and Austin were playing in the woods. They swung in a strong grapevine swing. They swung up into the blue sky and far out over the wide creek.

It was great fun. They smiled and laughed, and sang and whistled.

Then Austin said, "Let's play Indian."

"All right," said Abe. "Let's go to the cave. It's the best place in the world to play Indian."

They jumped to the ground and started toward the cave.

"You're right," said Austin. "That cave is the best place in the world to——"

Just then they heard a strange sound—a cry. Both boys stopped instantly.

"What was that?" whispered Austin.

"It sounded like a baby crying."

"A baby out here in the woods!" said Austin. "There couldn't be, Abe."

"Of course not, Austin. I said it sounded like one."

Then the boys heard the cry again.

"I can't understand it," said Austin.

"It comes from those bushes," said Abe. "I'm going to see what it is."

Austin seized Abe's arm. "Don't go over there!" he said. "It might be a panther. A panther can cry just like a child."

"But it might be something that is badly hurt," said Abe.

"I think it's a panther, Abe. I wouldn't go near those bushes."

"I'll wait till it cries again," said Abe.

"S—sh!" said Austin. "There it is!"

"I know it's something that is hurt," said Abe. "It has that kind of sound. I'm going!"

He ran toward the bushes. Austin waited just one minute, then he followed. He couldn't hang back when his chum went on.

The boys had reached the bushes when they heard the cry again. It was there—right by the place where they were standing.

They parted the branches and, as Abe had expected, there was something that was hurt. There lay a little dog with a broken leg.

"Poor doggie, poor doggie," said Abe.

"Poor doggie," said Austin.

The little dog looked at them. Then he cried again and again.

"Don't cry, doggie," said Abe. "I'll fix your leg. I know how."

He made a splint of stiff bark. Then he put the splint on the broken leg and tied it with strips of soft bark.

Austin watched him. "I wish I knew how to make a splint," he said.

"Father showed me," said Abe.

The poor little dog stopped crying and licked Abe's hand. That was his way of saying, "Thank you, little boy."

"Let's hide him in our cave," said Abe, "till he can walk."

"The very thing!" said Austin. "I'll go on ahead and make a bed of leaves."

Abe lifted the dog gently and carried him to the cave. Gently he lifted him on the bed of leaves and patted his head.

"I'll take care of him," said Abe. "I live nearer the cave than you do, Austin."

"I'd look after him if I could," said Austin. "You know that, don't you, Abe?"

"Of course I do," said Abe. "You would never let the poor dog go hungry any more than I would."

Then the boys patted the dog again and went away.

That evening Abe took food and water to the dog. He fed him every day. He gave him fresh water every day. He made a new bed of leaves every day. As soon as the dog could walk, Abe took him home. The broken leg was crooked, but it was strong.

Abe named the dog Honey, because he loved him dearly. And the dog loved Abe dearly and followed him everywhere.

Abe Learns by Watching

Mr. Lincoln came into the cabin and looked around. He saw Mrs. Lincoln getting supper. He saw Sarah helping, but he didn't see Abe.

"Where is Abe?" he asked.

"I sent him to Mrs. Brown's with some venison," said Mrs. Lincoln.

"When did he go?"

"At noon, just after dinner. He should be home by this time."

"Of course he should," said Mr. Lincoln. "He is playing in the woods."

"It's a long way to the Browns' and back, Thomas, and there are two steep hills to climb."

63

"I know, but he should have been here an hour ago. I want him to help me with a log. I can't lift it alone, and the fire is almost out."

Then Mr. Lincoln sat in front of the dying fire and waited. Ten minutes passed, fifteen, twenty.

Supper was ready, but everyone waited for Abe to come.

"He is always late," said Mr. Lincoln. "He thinks of nothing but play."

"He doesn't really play, Father," said Sarah. "He just stops to look at things."

"What things?" asked Mr. Lincoln.

"Oh, trees, clouds, grass and stones."

Mr. Lincoln frowned. "It's all nonsense," he said. "It's a bad habit."

Suddenly Mrs. Lincoln smiled. "I heard him whistle to Honey," she said. "He'll be here in a minute."

Sure enough, just then Abe and Honey came out of the dark woods. In another minute they were in the cabin, and Abe was hanging his cap on a peg.

"Mrs. Brown said she was much obliged for the venison," Abe said to his mother.

"You should have been home an hour ago," said his father.

"I didn't know it was so late. I was looking at something."

"You are always looking at something," said Mr. Lincoln angrily.

"I'll try not to be late again," said Abe.

"What were you looking at?" asked Sarah.

"That tall poplar tree on top of our hill."

"You've seen it at least a hundred times," said Mr. Lincoln.

"But I never noticed how it looked at night. It leans over, you know, Father."

"Well, what if it does?"

"Why, it leans right across the smoke that comes from Mr. Brown's chimney."

"Did you watch that for an hour?" asked Mr. Lincoln disgustedly.

"I watched it a long time. I wanted to see if the smoke was always back of the tree. And it was. It was pretty, too."

"I must look at it some night," said sweet Nancy Lincoln.

"There's no sense in looking at trees and smoke," said Mr. Lincoln. "You just waste time, and I want you to stop, Abe."

"I'll come straight home the next time."

"Supper is ready!" said Mrs. Lincoln.

"No supper till we put another log in the fireplace," said Mr. Lincoln. "Come along, Abe, and help me bring one in."

THE FIRE

One night a few weeks later a neighbor rushed to the Lincoln cabin. He didn't knock. He didn't take off his cap. He didn't speak to Mrs. Lincoln or Mr. Lincoln. He didn't speak to Sarah or Abe. He didn't tell them why he carried a large water bucket. He didn't say why the bucket was empty.

He just stood in the door and shouted, "Fire! Fire! Browns' cabin is on fire!"

"I'll be ready in one minute," said Mr. Lincoln, jumping to his feet.

"So will I," said Abe.

Now the Brown family lived some distance from the Lincolns, but that didn't make any difference. Settlers always helped one another if there was trouble.

So Mr. Lincoln seized a large bucket, and Mrs. Lincoln gave him his cap. Abe seized another bucket, and Sarah gave him his cap.

Then out ran Mr. Lincoln and the neighbor, and out ran Abe after them.

"I want to go, too!" cried Sarah.

"No, Sarah," said Mother, "you must stay here with me."

"But I've never seen a big fire," said Sarah. "Please let me go!"

"There's a creek to cross. Could you run over the log in the dark?"

Sarah hung her head. Mother went on: "The others will. Then they will climb the steep hills like rabbits, and leave you far behind."

"I'll stay here, Mother," said Sarah.

It was just as Mrs. Lincoln had said. The two men and Abe crossed the creek in the dark. And they ran across the log, too!

Then came a steep hill, and up they went like rabbits. Sometimes Abe slipped and fell, but he didn't mind that. He reached the top.

They could see the smoke plainly now, great clouds of it floating into the dark sky.

"Yes, it's Browns' cabin," said the neighbor. "There's no doubt of that."

"Not a bit!" said Mr. Lincoln. "Come on!"

"Wait!" said Abe. "There isn't any use in going farther."

The men were astonished. They turned and looked at Abe. He was standing near a large poplar tree and pointing to it.

"Look at this tree," he said. "Do you see any smoke back of it?"

"That's nonsense," said Mr. Lincoln. "Stop looking at that tree and come on."

"There's no use to go," said Abe. "The Browns' cabin isn't burning. The smoke from their chimney is always just back of this poplar tree. The tree bends over across it. I've seen it at night before."

"That is true," said Mr. Lincoln. "He told us about it some time ago."

Abe pointed to the smoke. "That smoke is south of this tree," he said. "It's a long way from the Browns' cabin."

70

"Then where is the fire?" asked the neighbor. "Whose cabin is burning?"

"Nobody's cabin is burning," said Abe. "That fire is in some woods on Mr. Brown's farm. He must be burning logs."

"Oh, I remember now," said the neighbor. "Mr. Brown told me he was going to burn some logs, but I forgot all about it."

Then he turned to Abe. "You've saved us a long hard trip, my boy," he said.

Then back down the hill went the two men and Abe. The men were silent. Abe was afraid that his father was angry.

At the foot of the hill the neighbor stopped. "Abe," he said, "how did you know that poplar tree leaned across the smoke from Mr. Brown's chimney?"

"I saw it one night, and I watched it so long that I was late for supper," said Abe.

"And I scolded him and told him to stop

watching things," said Mr. Lincoln. "I see now that I made a mistake."

"A big mistake, Thomas," said the neighbor. "Let Abe watch things, and he'll make one of the smartest men who ever came out of these Kentucky hills."

Mr. Lincoln didn't scold Abe for stopping to look at things—not for a long time.

Thank Honey

THE MILLER came to the door of his mill. "Abe," he called, "your corn meal is ready!" He waited for a moment, but Abe didn't come.

The miller called again. "Abe! Abe Lincoln! Your corn meal is ready."

He waited again for a moment, but still Abe didn't come.

The miller couldn't understand this. Abe often brought his father's corn to the mill, and he always waited until it was ground.

Once he had to wait all day. But he hadn't complained, and he hadn't gone home till the corn meal was ready.

No wonder the good miller was puzzled. He was just a bit angry, too. There were several men waiting to have their corn ground, and he must spend his time looking for Abe.

The men were talking outside. Now they were coming up to the mill. They didn't like this delay either. No doubt they were all in a hurry. They always wanted to get home before dark.

They were crossing a little footbridge close to the mill, and he could see their faces. To his great surprise not one of them looked angry. In fact, all of them seemed worried.

Their voices were anxious, too, when they spoke to him.

"Abe isn't around here," said one. "I saw him go into the woods a long time ago."

"So did I," said another. "His dog was with him."

"I saw him, too," said another.

"How long ago was that?" asked the miller.

"Oh, it was an hour or so, I guess."

"All of an hour," said the first man.

"Then I'm afraid he's lost," said the miller. "He's only seven years old."

"Only seven!" said the third man. "Does he bring his father's corn to the mill?"

"Yes," said the miller. "He rides a horse bareback, with the corn in a sack behind him. And he pays me every penny and takes the corn meal home."

"My boy couldn't do that," said the fourth man, "and he's eight."

"Abe is big for his age," said the second man.

"He is too smart to be lost," said the first man. "And he knows the forest."

"Yes, and he knows he ought to be back," said the miller.

"Then something must have happened to him," said the second man. "Bears with cubs are ugly just now."

"Wildcats and panthers are always ugly," said the first man.

"We must hunt for him," said the miller.

"Yes! Yes!" said the men.

"Lead the way," said the miller to the first man. "You saw where he entered the woods."

"Follow me!'" said the first man.

In single file they crossed the little footbridge and passed the great mill wheel. They went down the brook and through the clearing. They were now at the edge of the woods.

"This is where he went in," said the first man.

"Lead on," said the others.

But just then something happened—something that made every one of those men stop in his tracks.

A little dog came running out of the woods!

"Honey!" cried the miller.

"Honey!" cried the others.

It was indeed Honey. He barked sharply. He

leaped up to the miller's outstretched hand and touched it with his paw.

His eyes were troubled and anxious. Everything he did and the very sound of his bark said as plainly as words, "Abe's in trouble! Help!"

Honey ran to the other men and looked up

into their faces with his soft, anxious eyes. He barked sharply again and again.

Then he ran back into the woods. Suddenly he stopped and looked at the men again, and again he barked sharply. He was talking to them. He was saying, "Come on! Come on! Follow me!"

"He wants us to follow him," said one man. "See how he turns and looks at us."

"Something has happened to Abe," said another man, "and Honey has come to tell us."

"He'll lead us to Abe," said another man. "Come on!"

The men followed Honey. He led them far into the woods. At last he stopped at a cave. He looked at the men and barked. Then he ran into the cave.

The men followed Honey. The cave was not very light, and at first they had trouble seeing where they were going.

As soon as their eyes were used to the darkness, they walked faster. Soon they heard a boy's voice calling, "Help, help!"

"That sounds like Abe!" said the miller. "I know his voice."

"We're coming, Abe! We're coming!" shouted the men.

Very soon they found him. He could talk, but he couldn't move. He was held fast between two great rocks.

"Why, Abe," said the miller, "what has happened here?"

"I climbed up on this rock," said Abe. "Then all at once that large rock fell. I was caught between them and I couldn't move."

"The rock might have fallen on you," said one of the men.

The men worked carefully. Slowly they rolled the rock away and at last Abe was free.

He thanked the men for saving him.

"Don't thank us," they said. "Thank your dog, Honey!"

Then Honey barked and barked. That was his way of saying, "I brought these men here. I told them about you."

The men laughed at Honey and patted him. Abe patted him, too, but he didn't laugh.

"My goodness!" he cried. "What if that rock had fallen on Honey!"

The New Home in Indiana

Two TIRED horses came slowly along the road. On one was pretty dark-eyed Mrs. Nancy Lincoln. In front of her rode Sarah. Abe rode the other horse, with a great bundle of household goods tied on behind him. Mr. Lincoln walked beside the horses.

All day long they had traveled, and the day before, and the day before that, too.

"When will we come to the big, wide river?" asked Sarah.

"I thought we would make it by evening," said Mr. Lincoln, "but we can't. The horses are too tired. We'll camp in the first good place.

And here it is! A spring by the side of the road! This is good luck. Whoa! Whoa!"

In another minute everyone was busy. Mr. Lincoln fed and watered the horses. Then he gathered wood and made a fire. Mrs. Lincoln fried bacon and corncakes. Abe gathered leaves and made beds on the ground. Sarah took coverlets from the great bundle and laid them on the leaves.

By that time supper was ready, and the Lincoln family sat on a log and ate. Oh, how good the bacon and corncakes were! How cool the sparkling spring water was!

They talked about the home they had left on Knob Creek. They were all sorry to leave it.

"But our new home will be prettier," said Mother. "Our cabin will be on a little hill."

"Children," said Father, "there are walnut and hickory trees all over the place."

"I love walnuts," said Sarah.

"So do I," said Abe, "and I love hickory nuts, too. But I'm sorry I have to leave Austin."

"Austin can visit us," said Mother.

"And best of all," said Father, "corn grows better in Indiana. So I'll make more money than I did in Kentucky."

"Oh, I'm sure you will, Thomas," said Mother. "And now, children, it's time for bed."

"Will you keep the fire burning all night?" asked Sarah.

"Yes, indeed," said Father. "There are many wild animals in these woods."

"May I help watch?" Abe asked.

"I may call you later. I'll watch first."

The others got ready for bed. It took only a moment. They just rolled up in their covers, clothes and all, and were soon fast asleep.

Suddenly Abe heard his father call him. It was his turn to watch, so he jumped out from his covers and went to the fire.

"Why, this isn't any fire at all," he said. Then he piled on wood until he had it blazing.

"No beasts will come near this fire," he said. "They can see it far away."

Then he piled on more wood and kept the fire blazing for a long time.

Suddenly he noticed that the fire was going out. He looked for wood, but there was no more. He was frightened.

"What shall I do?" he thought. He didn't dare go into the dark forest for wood.

The blaze went out. The fire was only smoking now. All around was a wall of darkness—black, black darkness.

And now in this wall of black Abe saw two green spots of light—the eyes of some wild animal! They were coming toward him! Nearer and nearer they came!

"Father!" he called. "Father! Father!"

"Wake up! Wake up!" his father said.

Abe opened his eyes and sat up. It was just daylight. The fire was burning. Bacon and corn-cakes were frying.

"Why, I thought I let the fire go out," said Abe. "I saw two green eyes watching me."

"You had a bad dream," said Mother.

"Didn't I watch the fire at all?"

"No," said Father, "your mother and I did."

"I'm glad it was a dream," said Abe, "but I learned how to keep a fire burning all night."

"How?" Father asked.

"A low fire, no blaze, and just a little wood at a time."

"That boy learns in his sleep," said Father.

They all laughed. Then Abe crawled out of his covers, and Sarah crawled out of hers. They washed at the spring and combed their hair. Then they were ready for breakfast.

Again the Lincoln family sat on the log and ate bacon and corncakes. Then on they went, toward the beautiful Ohio River.

INTO THE WILDERNESS

A ferryboat took the Lincolns, horses and all, across the Ohio River. When they reached the other shore, they were in Indiana. But they were still far from their new home.

Mr. Lincoln hired a big wagon and hitched up his horses. The others threw the bundles in and sat on them. Then off they drove into the wilderness.

Mrs. Lincoln and the children had never seen such a dense forest. There was no end to it.

They had to travel slowly, for the road wasn't much more than a path. At times Mr. Lincoln had to cut away tree branches so the wagon could pass on.

Of course Abe helped. He knew how to handle an ax because he had helped his father in Kentucky.

The trail was very rough. Sometimes the wagon bumped over big roots. Then the whole family would bounce into the air.

But that didn't worry the Lincolns. The more they bounced, the more they laughed.

"It's fun to bounce," said Abe. "I like it."

"So do I," said Sarah.

Now a wide creek had to be crossed. The children watched the water creeping up, closer and closer to the wagon bed, and were frightened.

Mother didn't seem to like it, either. "Thomas!" she called. "The water will come into the wagon!"

"Oh, that won't hurt anything," said Mr. Lincoln. "We can dry everything in the sun."

"Why, of course we can," said Mother. "I didn't think of that."

"And your feet won't melt if the water does cover them," said Father. "You're neither sugar nor salt."

"That's true," said Mother. "We'll just play we are wading in the creek, children."

What fun those two children had then! The water did come into the wagon, up to their ankles, and they could wade sitting still.

After that, they were eager to cross creeks.

So on they went, farther and farther into

the great wilderness. On they went, bumping, bouncing, wading and laughing.

At last they reached Mr. Lincoln's land. There was no clearing, no cabin, no shelter of any kind. There was nothing but the dense, dense forest.

The children had no time to be afraid of Indians or wild animals. They had to go to work at once.

Mr. Lincoln and Abe cut down small trees and made a shed with the poles. It wasn't much of a home, but at least it was a shelter from rain and snow.

Then came the new log cabin. Large trees had to be chopped down and made into logs. The logs had to be cut certain lengths. Large stumps had to be pulled or burned.

It was all hard work, and the weather was

cold and wet. All winter long, on every clear day, Abe worked with his father.

Mrs. Lincoln and Sarah had to find the food. Mrs. Lincoln could shoot almost as well as Mr. Lincoln. Sometimes she shot a deer. Sometimes she came back with squirrels or rabbits.

The front of the shed had been left open, and in this opening the Lincolns had their fire. And here they did their cooking.

At last the cabin was almost finished. The floor wasn't laid and the windows and door weren't made, but the Lincolns moved in anyway. It was better than the shed. Mother said they could get along for a while, until Father had finished clearing land for a cornfield.

Mother liked the new cabin because it was in such a beautiful place. It stood on a slight elevation in the midst of large forest trees. It was shaded by walnut and hickory trees. Near by were papaw and sassafras trees.

There were wild grapevines and spice bushes and many kinds of wild berries.

All this delighted Mrs. Lincoln. "Thomas," she said, "you have chosen a beautiful spot for our home."

She hung a bearskin over the open doorway and spread deerskins on the dirt floor.

In the evening, after the day's work was done, the Lincoln family sat before a blazing fire in the large fireplace.

Sometimes Sarah and Abe ate walnuts or hickory nuts. Sometimes they just sat still and listened to Father tell Indian stories until Mother said, "Time for bed, children!"

Then up the pegs in the wall went Abe. He slept in the loft on a pile of sweet-smelling leaves, covered with a thick wool cover. He had no pillow, but he had a bearskin over him and he was warm and happy.

All of the Lincolns were happy together. The

cabin was a dear place to them. It was their home, and they loved it.

MOTHER PLANS FOR ABE

Mrs. Lincoln liked the new home in Indiana, except for one thing. There was no school in the Pigeon Creek Settlement, and Nancy Lincoln wanted her children to go to school.

She had gone to school herself when she was a girl, and she could read and write. She had learned to love good books, and she wanted Sarah and Abe to love them.

But what could she do? There wasn't a school within ten miles.

"Well," she said, "we will have school here at home, and I will be the schoolmaster."

The children hadn't gone to school in Kentucky very long, and they had forgotten all they had learned. So Mrs. Lincoln began with their

letters. Then she taught them spelling and reading and a little arithmetic.

She told them Bible stories and read the Bible
to them.

She taught them to be honest.

She taught them good manners.

Abe learned to take off his coonskin cap when
he entered a cabin. He learned to stand until
older persons were seated.

Both children learned to say, "Thank you"
and "Good morning" and "Good night."

Indeed, Sarah and Abe had such good manners that, later on, other settlers liked to have
their children visit the Lincolns.

The school went on. Mrs. Lincoln gave the
children as much time as she could, but she
was too busy to give them as much time as they
really needed.

But she found out several things. She found
that, while both children were smart and learned

quickly, Abe was the one who really loved to study. So she made up her mind to one thing: Abe should go to school.

Mr. Lincoln didn't agree with her. He had never gone to school himself, and he couldn't read or write.

"You've taught Abe to read and write," he said. "That's enough for any boy who is going to work in the fields all his life."

"No, Thomas, it isn't enough. Abe is not like other boys. He is more serious, and he asks smart questions about things."

"He asks too many questions. I tell him to get to work."

"Because you can't answer him and neither can I," said Mrs. Lincoln. "And that's just the reason he should have a real teacher—someone who can tell him what he wants to know."

"Well, there isn't any school near enough, Nancy, so that settles it."

"No, Thomas, it doesn't. There is a way: we'll move near a school."

"And begin all over again? Build a new cabin and clear new land?"

"Yes," said that determined young mother, "we'll begin all over again."

Just then Abe came into the cabin.

"Abe," said Mother, "we are talking about sending you to school."

"You don't want to go, do you?" asked Father. "You'd rather work in the field, wouldn't you?"

"No," said Abe. "I'd rather go to school and work with books."

"Abe, you shall go to school next winter if I live," said Nancy Lincoln.

But Nancy Lincoln didn't live. She died in the fall of 1818.

Changes in the Family

ONE NIGHT a little girl and two boys sat in the Lincoln cabin and looked into the fire. They were alone in the cabin. And the great dark forest was like a wall of darkness that shut them in and held them fast.

Abe was now ten and a half, and Sarah was past twelve. The boy who was staying with them was several years older.

For a long time they didn't say anything. They just sat on stools and looked into the fire. All of them seemed unhappy.

At last Sarah said, "It's lonesome here."

"It's mighty lonesome," said Abe.

"I guess you miss your mother," said the older boy kindly.

"Yes, I do, Cousin Dennis," said Sarah.

"So do I," said Abe.

"I miss her, too," said Dennis. "Look how she had me come here and live when my mother died. And she was always good to me, too."

"She was good to everyone," said Sarah.

"No one else could be so good," said Abe.

"I'm glad you are here, Dennis," said Sarah. "I'm sorry the cabin isn't as clean as Mother kept it." She looked at the untidy room.

"You work too hard, Sarah," said Dennis. "I wish I could help you more."

"I bring in the water and wood," said Abe.

"You both do all you can," Sarah said quickly. "You have too much work yourselves since Father went away."

"We are trying to finish that rail fence before he gets back," Dennis said.

"We want to surprise him," said Abe.

"He said he wouldn't be gone long, but it's been a month today," said Sarah.

"That isn't long," said Abe. "He had to walk, and it's a hundred miles to Knob Creek."

"And a hundred miles back," Dennis added with a laugh.

But Sarah didn't even smile. "Anyway, I think it's queer he went away and left us alone," she said.

"It is queer," said Dennis.

Abe didn't say anything, but he thought it was queer, too.

Then they stopped talking and looked into the fire again. It burned low.

"It's time to go to bed," said Sarah.

"Good night," said Dennis, and up the pegs he went to the loft.

"Good night," said Abe, and up he followed Dennis.

Sarah went to bed in the untidy room below. All was quiet in the cabin.

Now the forest began to speak its language of sounds and warnings. An owl hooted, and Sarah hid her head under her quilt.

A wildcat screamed, and Abe crept closer to Dennis in their bed of leaves.

WHAT THE BIG WAGON BROUGHT

Another day went by, and then another and another. Still Mr. Lincoln didn't return, and the three children were alone.

But they went on with their work, the boys in the woods splitting rails and Sarah in the cabin doing housework.

She tried hard to get good meals for Abe and Dennis, but nothing she cooked was just right. The mush was too thin. The corncakes were too hard. The meat was either burned or raw.

She tried to wash the heavy bedclothes, but she couldn't lift them. She tried to sew and mend, but the clothes didn't look right.

She was discouraged. Every day she cried and cried.

Then suddenly everything was changed. One morning a big wagon came through the woods to the Lincoln cabin. The wagon was drawn by four horses!

Out of the cabin rushed Sarah. Out of the woods rushed Dennis and Abe. Out of the wagon jumped Thomas Lincoln!

"Children," he said. "I have brought you a present from Kentucky. I have brought you a new mother."

A tall pretty woman jumped from the wagon and ran toward them. She had fair curly hair and the sweetest smile.

"Children!" she cried. "Children!" With that she hugged them and kissed them. She told

them they were her children now and she had come to take care of them.

"You will be just like my own children to me," she said. "You are all about the same age, and you will have a good time together."

Then this lively lady turned toward the wagon and called, "John! Matilda! Sarah!"

At once the three Johnston children jumped from the wagon and smiled at Abe and Sarah and Dennis.

And Abe and Sarah and Dennis smiled at John and Matilda and Sarah Johnston.

"Now, children," said Mrs. Lincoln, "please take everything out of the wagon and carry it into the cabin."

Six happy young people began to unload the big wagon. There were great bundles of featherbeds, pillows, quilts, wool coverlets, sheets, towels and clothing. The Lincoln children and Dennis were amazed to see so many things.

"The bureau next!" called Mrs. Lincoln. "And do please be careful!"

"My goodness!" said Sarah Lincoln. "A bureau! I never saw one before."

John, Dennis and Abe carried it into the cabin. Sarah would have thought they were carrying eggs—they were so careful.

"It's beautiful," said Abe.

"It makes the cabin look fine," said Dennis.

"Wait till you see the chairs," said Matilda. "They have backs."

"Backs!" cried Sarah and Abe and Dennis.

They ran to the wagon, and soon six chairs stood in the cabin—six chairs with backs.

"Oh! How beautiful!" cried Sarah Lincoln. "It's the finest cabin on Pigeon Creek now. Isn't it, boys?"

"It is," said Abe.

"It is," Dennis agreed.

How that new mother worked! Here, there

and everywhere, just like the general of an army. And she had her army working, too.

Clean bedclothes went on the beds. Dishes, knives, forks and spoons were scoured. Pots and pans were scoured. The table, benches and stools were scrubbed. Soon everything was so clean it just couldn't be any cleaner.

Next, Mrs. Lincoln began on Sarah and Abe. Soon they were so clean they just couldn't be any cleaner.

Then she gave Sarah a pretty new dress. She gave Abe new shirts and trousers. She gave them both new shoes—not moccasins—shoes. She made two sad children so happy they didn't know themselves.

That night Abe and Dennis slept on a feather-bed in the loft. Clean pillows were under their heads and clean quilts covered them. How happy and comfortable they were! How Abe loved this new mother!

And that wasn't all. Mrs. Sarah Johnston Lincoln told Mr. Thomas Lincoln that she wanted a wooden floor, windows and a door. And she told him so plainly he couldn't misunderstand, so he just went to work and made them.

He was really a good carpenter, and now he had three boys to help him. So it wasn't long until there was a beautiful clean floor and a door and windows.

Never again was that cabin a lonely place. Six children helped with the work. Six children laughed and talked. Six children popped corn, roasted apples and cracked nuts.

But best of all to Sarah and Abe was to have that kind new mother.

MRS. LINCOLN LOOKS AHEAD

"Thomas," said Abe's stepmother, "Abe must go to school."

"But he knows his letters, Sarah, and he can read and spell a little."

"Very little," said Mrs. Lincoln. "He hasn't been to school since you moved to Indiana, and that was three years ago."

"There wasn't any school near enough."

"There is now, right here on Pigeon Creek. And Abe ought to go. He is eleven years old."

"Oh, Abe is getting along all right. He can work as well as a man," said Thomas Lincoln.

"Work isn't everything, Thomas."

"It's enough for Abe. He'll always be a farm hand. He can't do anything else."

"You can't tell me that, Thomas Lincoln! Abe is smart. He loves books and he remembers everything. He can tell every story he ever heard."

"I know he can do that," said Thomas. "He can even tell what the preacher said at meeting." Then Thomas laughed and laughed.

"What are you laughing at?" asked Sarah.

"Why," said Thomas, "yesterday that boy got up on a stump in the cornfield and preached."

"Preached? You don't mean to say Abe preached?"

"I do," said Thomas. "He thought he was alone, but I was in the woods and I hid behind a tree and listened." Then Mr. Lincoln laughed again.

"Go on! Go on!" said Sarah.

"Well," said Thomas, "Abe acted exactly like the preacher. He made motions like the preacher. He coughed like the preacher. And he actually preached like him, too."

"How could he preach?" asked Mrs. Lincoln. "He didn't have anyone to preach to."

"He preached to the cornstalks, Sarah. And he preached last Sunday's sermon!"

"Did he remember it?"

"He remembered it better than I did."

"Abe is the smartest boy I know," said Sarah.

"He's too smart," said Thomas. "He can imitate the preacher exactly, and he's funny when he does it. But the preaching has to stop. It takes him away from his work."

"Thomas, let Abe go to school this winter. He wants to learn. He'll study hard."

"I can't spare him this winter, Sarah. Some

land must be cleared for a new field. We need more bread for such a large family."

"I know we do, Thomas, but the land can be cleared in the spring. Abe can stop school when you are ready for him. You can't work through the heavy snows, anyway."

"That's true," said Mr. Lincoln. "But I haven't any money, Sarah. I can't pay a schoolmaster."

"I'll pay him myself," said Mrs. Lincoln, "with my chicken money."

"You seem determined, Sarah."

"I am determined, Thomas. Abe must have a chance to go to school."

A Busy
All-Round Boy

THERE WERE now several families in the Pigeon Creek neighborhood. Each family had several children, and the parents had decided that it was time to hire a schoolmaster. All the families together could afford to pay one.

So these settlers had built a school. It was a log house with one room.

At one end of this room there was a large fireplace which was filled with blazing logs in the winter. This made that end of the room too warm and left the other end too cold.

Abe didn't mind that. He was used to cold at home, and so were the other pupils.

The schoolroom wasn't very light, either. It had only two small windows, and they were made of greased paper.

Abe didn't mind that, and neither did the others. That was what they had at home, if they had windows at all.

The pupils sat on benches without backs. They had to sit on those benches for hours and hours. The children's backs grew tired.

But Abe didn't mind that. None of the pupils did. They all sat on stools and benches at home. Of course the Lincoln family had chairs now, but not enough to go around. So Abe always used a stool.

At first Abe was in the class with younger pupils. Some of them were only six years old, and Abe was eleven!

But he didn't care—he was determined to learn. He studied so hard and learned so fast he was soon in the class of older children.

Every night he studied his lessons while his brother and sisters and cousin were playing.

Mr. Lincoln didn't like to see Abe study at home, but he couldn't say much because Mrs. Lincoln wouldn't let him. She wouldn't allow the other children to bother Abe, either.

"Abe is studying," she would say, and that settled it.

The Lincolns couldn't afford to burn candles every night, so Abe studied by firelight. He

didn't have a pencil, so he used a partly-burned stick of wood. He didn't have paper, so he used a wooden shovel.

He was determined to learn.

Mrs. Lincoln was proud of Abe. She told the neighbors how hard he studied, and they told their neighbors.

Before long everyone in the Pigeon Creek Settlement knew about it, and they all tried to help the boy.

They couldn't do much because they were all poor, and few of them could read or write. But if they had books they loaned them to Abe.

Abe was glad to have these books. He would walk miles and miles to borrow a book and miles and miles to return it.

He read every book again and again until he knew it almost by heart. Then he would tell the stories to his good stepmother, who listened eagerly to every word.

So Abe went on studying, reading, learning. And always back of him stood that splendid stepmother, Sarah Johnston Lincoln.

"Abe is studying," she would say. And that settled it.

AT THE END OF EACH ROW

When spring came, Abe had to stop school. His father needed him to help make a new field.

The Lincolns now had a large family. Such a large family meant more bread; more bread meant more wheat; more wheat meant a new field.

A new field meant the cutting down of many giant forest trees. Every tree that fell meant a great heavy log to cut and a great heavy stump to dig up and burn.

Such hard work kept them all busy—Mr. Lincoln, John, Dennis and Abe. At daylight they were up and at work; at sundown they went home. Then they ate supper and went to bed— all except Abe.

Tired as he was, he studied every night, sometimes till midnight and past midnight.

He even took books to the field and read while he was plowing.

The ground was so rough that plowing was hard on the horses. It made them tired to pull the heavy plow. They had to rest at the end of each row. While they rested, Abe read. Not one minute was wasted.

Sometimes he worked arithmetic problems. He always carried a partly-burned stick in his pocket, and he wrote on fence rails and ends of logs.

Mr. Lincoln didn't like this, but what could he say? The horses had to rest, didn't they?

Sometimes Abe would make a speech, which always delighted John and Dennis. It delighted others, too. Farm boys in near-by fields would leave their plows and come running to hear Abe speak. He always told funny stories, and the boys would laugh and laugh.

Mr. Lincoln didn't like this, either. "It won't do," he said. "You are taking the boys away from their work."

"They work all the harder afterward," said Abe. "They laugh and forget they are tired."

"But I don't want you making speeches," said Mr. Lincoln. "It's time wasted. You can't be a lawyer."

"Maybe I can some day," said Abe. "I'd like to be a lawyer."

"That's nonsense, Abe. You'll never have a chance to study law."

"I'll make the chance," said Abe.

"You can't do it," said Mr. Lincoln. "I can't help you; I'm too poor. All you can ever do is farm work."

"But I want to work with books," said Abe.

"Books!" said his father. "Always books! What is all this studying going to do for you? What do you think you are going to be?"

"Why," said Abe, "I'm going to be President." Then Abe laughed. John laughed and Dennis laughed and Mr. Lincoln laughed, too. It was a good joke. Abe Lincoln, President! Ha, ha, ha!

BORROWED BOOKS

New settlers moved to the Pigeon Creek Settlement. They came in big wagons and built log cabins in the woods. They cleared fields for corn and wheat. They made vegetable gardens close to their cabins.

The old settlers went to see their new neighbors and told them about the church and the school. Then, nine times out of ten, they boasted about Abe Lincoln.

119

"He reads books," they said. "He reads by the light of the fire, and he reads till midnight and past midnight."

"Till midnight!" said the new settlers. "Till past midnight! Why, we never heard anything like it."

"We lend him our books," the old settlers said. "He will walk miles to borrow them."

"Will he return them?" the new settlers asked.

"Yes," said the old settlers, "he always returns them. And he brings them back as good as they were when he borrowed them."

Then the new settlers looked through their things. If they found a book, they loaned it to Abe, who always returned it. And the book was always as good as it was when he borrowed it.

Once Abe borrowed *The Life of George Washington*. He was delighted with this book, and he made up his mind then and there that he would try to be like Washington—always honest and always loyal to his country.

He read on and on, till midnight and past midnight. Then he had to go to bed, but he took the book to the loft with him.

"I'll read it in the morning," he said to himself, "before the others are up."

He put the book in a crack between two logs. Then he went to sleep.

That night there was a snowstorm, and the snow blew into the loft through the wide cracks. Abe woke up early. What was this? Snow on his bed! Snow on the floor! And worst of all, snow on *The Life of George Washington!*

Abe felt very bad. The pages were not wet, but the book cover was ruined. He knew he should pay for the book. But he had no money.

So what did Abe do? Did he pretend he had lost the book? Did he pretend someone had taken it?

121

No indeed! Abe took the book straight to the owner and explained the ruined cover. Then he offered to work for the man until the book was paid for.

"Very well," said the man. "You may work three days for me, husking corn."

Abe worked the three days from sunrise till sunset. And then he had a big surprise. The man gave him the book!

Abe was delighted. He took the book home and read it again and again. Each time he read it he became more and more determined to be like General George Washington, twice President of the United States.

HAVING FUN

Abe loved his books, but he wasn't reading every minute when he wasn't working in the fields or woods. He liked to tell stories and ask riddles. He liked nothing better than playing good jokes on other people.

One year his mother finished her spring house-cleaning early. She was proud of the cabin, for she had whitewashed the ceiling.

"I suppose that smoke from the fireplace will make the ceiling dirty again very soon," she sighed. "Anyway, let's all try to keep it clean as long as we can."

A few weeks later one of the neighbors came to the Lincoln cabin early in the morning. His wife was sick, and he wanted Mrs. Lincoln to go home with him and care for her. He had brought along his little boy, David.

"I'd be obliged if David could stay here today," the neighbor said.

Mrs. Lincoln left at once with the neighbor, and David stayed with the Lincolns. Mr. Lincoln was away, but the children could take care of themselves and David, too.

When Abe came to the cabin for dinner, he found David playing outside the door. There had been some rain and the yard was muddy. The little boy's feet were muddy, too.

"Wipe off your feet before you come in," Matilda called to David.

Then and there Abe had an idea. "Leave the mud on your feet, David," he said, "and let me carry you into the cabin."

Abe picked up the little boy and took him inside. "I have thought of a good joke to play on Mother," he said.

Then, while the other children watched and laughed, Abe held David upside down and let him "walk" on the ceiling. The muddy footprints looked very funny!

Late that evening the neighbor brought Mrs. Lincoln home. His wife was feeling much better, and she wanted David to come home with his father.

After the neighbor and David left, Abe began to read. Nobody said a word about the tracks on the ceiling, but everyone was waiting for Mrs. Lincoln to notice them.

At first she was too busy finding out how the girls had managed without her. When at last she saw the tracks, she gasped.

"Oh, the ceiling!" she wailed. "What happened to the clean ceiling?"

She looked at Abe. He was hiding behind his book, but he couldn't keep from laughing. Then the other children laughed, and finally Mrs. Lincoln laughed, too.

Abe did no more reading that evening. He was busy washing mud off the ceiling. He didn't care. After all, he didn't have a chance to play such a good joke very often.

Sometimes Abe had fun with the other boys who lived on Pigeon Creek. He played games with them, he ran races, he jumped, he lifted weights and wrestled.

These boys were all farm boys. They worked in the fields and woods, and they were very strong. But Abe Lincoln was the strongest of them all.

He could run faster than any of them. "That is because my legs are so long," he said.

He could jump higher than any of them. "That is because my neck is so long," he said.

He could move bigger logs than any of them. "That is because my arms are so long," he said.

He could throw any of them when they wrestled. "That is because my hands are so big," he said.

Abe always gave reasons like those. He never bragged about himself. The boys liked him for that. They liked him, too, because he never cheated and because he was fair to each side.

They saw that they could always trust Abe, so they made him their leader.

Now, these boys didn't study very hard when they were in school, and they didn't read books between times or at any time.

"What good will books do us?" they said. "We'll have to work in the fields all our lives."

When they talked this way, Abe didn't argue with them. Instead, he usually told them a story. The other boys couldn't understand why Abe liked to read, but they could understand his stories. They never guessed that Abe found many of his stories in books.

The Preacher
Comes

IT WAS LATE in the afternoon, but Abe was still working in the forest. He was chopping down trees, and he had been working all day.

He was tired and wanted to stop. He looked at the sun. No, he couldn't stop yet. The sun was still above the treetops. Abe could tell the time by the sun as well as anyone else could by a clock.

Now Abe was alone in the woods. He might have stopped work. There was no one to see and no one to tell. But Abe was honest. He kept right on chopping.

"Abe! Abe!" someone called.

"Here I am!" called Abe.

A minute later his sister Sarah came down the path.

"Abe," she said, "guess who has come!"

"I can't guess," said Abe. "Who is it?"

"It's the preacher!" Sarah said. "He's going to stay for supper and all night."

"I'm glad," said Abe. "I like to hear him talk. But I can't stop work for an hour or so."

"Father said that you should stop now," said Sarah.

"Stop now!" said Abe. "I can't understand why I should stop early."

"I can't either," said Sarah, "but that's what Father said. He wants you to come right away. And Mother said you should wash before you come into the cabin."

"I always do, don't I?"

"Sometimes you forget, Abe."

"Maybe I do sometimes."

Then Abe swung his ax over his shoulder and went home with Sarah.

He washed extra well. He combed his hair extra well. Then he went into the cabin.

"Here is Abe," said Mrs. Lincoln, but she didn't smile.

"The preacher has something to say to you, Abe," said Mr. Lincoln, and he didn't smile.

"Good evening, Abe," said the preacher, and he didn't smile either.

Abe couldn't understand. The preacher had always joked and laughed with him before.

"Pastor," said Mr. Lincoln, "tell Abe just why you came."

The preacher looked at Abe. "Abe," he said, "I heard that you had been making fun of me. You preached and you made the boys laugh."

"Oh—oh, yes," said Abe.

"You coughed just as I do," said the preacher, "and the boys laughed at that."

"Oh—oh, yes," said poor Abe again.

"And you stood as I do, one leg out, the other leg in. Didn't you?"

"Yes, sir," said Abe.

"And, worst of all, you blew your nose as I do. Didn't you?"

"Yes, sir," said Abe. "But really I wasn't making fun of you, sir. I was just trying to preach."

"That was it," said Mrs. Lincoln. "Abe wanted to preach, and so, of course, he tried to copy you. He didn't know any other way."

"Sarah, you are always making excuses for Abe," said Mr. Lincoln.

"You laughed at Abe's preaching yourself, Thomas," said Mrs. Lincoln.

Thomas didn't know what to say to this. So he said, "Never mind, we won't talk about that." Then he turned to the preacher and said, "Pastor, I'm going to whip Abe for making fun of you."

"Thomas!" said Mrs. Lincoln. "Don't whip Abe! He didn't know he was doing wrong."

Mr. Lincoln didn't answer her. He took a leather strap from a peg.

"Abe," he said, "go out in the yard."

Abe crossed to the door. Mr. Lincoln followed him.

Suddenly a strong hand seized Mr. Lincoln's arm and took the leather strap.

"Don't touch the boy!" said the preacher. "I was only joking. I thought you knew that. Abe was really helping me when he tried to preach for the other boys."

"Helping you!" said Mr. Lincoln. "I don't understand."

"Why," said the preacher, "every one of those boys came to meeting last Sunday."

"They just went to make fun of you," said Mr. Lincoln.

"Of course," said the preacher. "But they

133

stayed, and some of them joined the church. I never held such a meeting. It was splendid."

"Well, well!" said Mr. Lincoln, "I'm surprised to hear that."

"I'm not surprised," said Mrs. Lincoln.

Abe didn't say anything. He didn't know what to say.

The preacher put his arm around Abe. "My boy," he said, "just go on preaching. Your jokes will do a lot of good in the world."

Abe Thinks
of Others

ONE DAY Abe went to the creek to fish. He didn't
fish with his hands now. He had a pole and line.

On the bank stood four boys. They were looking at something on the ground, and they were
laughing and shouting.

"I wonder what they are looking at," Abe
said to himself.

He went up to them and looked over their
heads. There, on the ground, was a large mud
turtle. Its shell had been broken. It was trying
to crawl, but it couldn't. It could only jerk and
quiver.

Abe saw that it was suffering, and he was

135

very angry. He knew that one of the boys had hurt it.

He pushed the boys back. "Stand back!" he said. "Let me have that turtle!"

"You can't have it!" said the largest boy. "It's my turtle. I found it."

"You broke its back, didn't you?" said Abe.

"Yes, I did," said the boy. "I wanted to see how it would crawl. I knew it would look funny."

"I wonder how you would crawl if I broke your back," said Abe. "I wonder if you would look funny."

The boy saw that Abe was very angry, and he was afraid of him. He knew how strong Abe was, because he had seen him wrestle. So he didn't say another word. He didn't laugh again, either.

The other boys stopped laughing, too. They were all afraid of Abe.

Abe picked up the turtle gently and put it into the creek.

Then Abe said, "Boys, God made that mud turtle. Do you think he wanted you to hurt it?"

The boys hung their heads.

"Do you think God would laugh at its poor broken back?"

The boys still looked at the ground. They were ashamed to look at Abe.

He went on: "Do you think God laughed when it quivered and jerked?"

There was silence for a moment, then a boy said, "I am sorry I laughed, Abe."

"I am sorry I laughed," said another boy.

"I didn't know a turtle suffered," said the largest boy. "It's nothing but an animal."

"Animals suffer just as much as we do," said Abe. "I found a dog once, with a broken leg. It was crying just like a child. No child could have suffered more."

"I'll never hurt an animal again," said the largest boy. "If I do you may lick me, Abe."

"That is just what I will do," said Abe.

He meant what he said, and the boys knew that he meant it.

HUNTING WILD TURKEYS

One day Abe was busy with his ax, splitting some rails. Two boys came along, with their guns over their shoulders.

"Where are you going?" Abe asked.

"Hunting," the bigger boy answered. "There are lots of wild turkeys in the woods."

"Why don't you get a gun and come with us?" asked the other boy.

Abe leaned on his ax and thought for a moment. He didn't know whether he wanted to go hunting or not. He knew how to use a gun, but he didn't enjoy hunting. He hated to kill or even hurt any living thing. Still it would be fun to be with the other boys.

At last he said, "I've never hunted turkeys, but I'd like to go with you. I must finish splitting these rails first, though."

The boys waited. It wasn't long before the rails were all split and piled up neatly.

Then Abe got a gun from the cabin and went with the boys. They were careful where they stepped. They knew that any noise would frighten the birds and animals.

They had not gone far when Abe stopped suddenly. Without saying a word, he pointed to two turkeys feeding in the underbrush.

"You shoot, Abe," one boy whispered. "You saw them first."

Abe took careful aim and fired. One turkey toppled over, and the other flew off.

"You got it!" shouted the boys, as they ran toward the turkey. Abe felt as if his feet were rooted to the ground. He didn't want to look at the bird he had shot.

"Come on, Abe!" called one of the boys. "See what a big turkey you shot. I'll bet it weighs at least twenty pounds."

Abe walked slowly to the turkey. The wings of the big bird were still flapping feebly.

"It's too bad we didn't shoot the other one," the bigger boy said, "but turkeys usually stay in flocks. There should be others around if the shot didn't frighten them too much."

"Pick up your bird, Abe," said the other boy.

"Probably we'll have to do some walking before we find any more turkeys."

Abe knew that his mother would be glad to have the turkey. His father often shot different kinds of wild game to help out on the food supply. This was the first time that Abe had ever killed anything.

He had to make himself pick up the turkey. Its wings flapped a few times against his shoulder. Then they were still.

Abe walked along behind the other boys. They saw several flocks of turkeys. Before long Abe's friends had shot two turkeys apiece. Abe did not fire another shot.

When the boys urged him to shoot, he just shook his head. "I can't do it," he said. "This is the first time I ever killed anything with a gun. I hope that it is the last time, too."

After that when other boys went into the woods with their guns, Abe stayed home. He knew that sometimes it was necessary to kill wild game for food, but he couldn't do it. If the family needed wild game, someone else would have to shoot it.

AN ACCIDENT

Another time Abe was going into the woods to chop down a tree.

"May I go with you, Abe?" Matilda called from the doorway.

Mrs. Lincoln put her hand on Matilda's shoulder before Abe could answer. "Not today, Matilda," she said. "I need you to help me. Besides, I don't want you bothering Abe while he is working with a sharp ax."

Abe liked to be out in the woods. He liked to chop down trees. He sang at the top of his voice as he lifted the ax over his head. He worked and worked.

142

Abe was singing so loudly that he didn't hear Matilda come up behind him. Now, Matilda knew just what she was going to do. She had watched her brothers play.

She crept up softly behind Abe. He had just raised his ax high over his head. Quick as a cat, Matilda leaped on Abe's back. She put one hand on each of his shoulders. Her knees were in the middle of Abe's back.

Abe whirled around, still holding the ax. Matilda tumbled to the ground. As she fell, her knee hit the sharp blade of the ax!

Abe's face grew pale when he saw the blood running down Matilda's leg. He dropped the ax and bent over his sister.

"Oh, Matilda, I've cut your knee!" he said.

Matilda was quite a big girl, but she couldn't keep from crying now. "Oh, Abe, it hurts! It hurts!" she sobbed.

Abe could see that the cut was fairly deep. "We should bandage your knee and get you home," he said.

His hands were shaking as he tore a strip off his shirt and bound up the knee. He felt very sorry for Matilda.

"I know it hurts awfully," he said. "But I'm sure it will be all right."

Matilda had stopped crying now. "Don't look so worried, Abe. It isn't your fault that I

144

got hurt. It's mine. I shouldn't have come to the woods and surprised you."

Abe tried to smile. "Well, I can't help being worried. I hate to see anyone get hurt. I'll carry you home now."

Abe walked carefully. He didn't want the cut on Matilda's knee to start bleeding again. As he walked, he began to worry about his mother. If she saw him carrying Matilda, she would be frightened, he knew.

"Matilda," said Abe when they came in sight of the cabin, "do you think you could walk the rest of the way? I know your knee hurts, but I don't want to scare Mother."

"Oh, yes," said Matilda. "I'm sure I can walk now. I should have thought about frightening Mother, myself. You always think about others, Abe. I wish I could be like that."

"Well, I'm older than you are," said Abe, as he put Matilda on her feet.

Matilda leaned on Abe, and together they went toward the cabin. When Mrs. Lincoln saw them coming, she rushed to meet them. She was half angry and half worried. Matilda had disobeyed her, and she didn't like that. At the same time she was worried when she saw that Abe was coming home with Matilda.

"Matilda," she said, "I told you not to go to the woods——"

"Please don't scold her, Mother," said Abe. "She just didn't think. She has had an accident, and I think perhaps she has already been punished enough."

When Mrs. Lincoln saw the cut on Matilda's knee, she agreed with Abe. She didn't scold Matilda, but gently took care of the gash.

"You are lucky to have a brother like Abe," she said to Matilda. "He always understands how the other person feels."

A Spelling Match

"ARE YOU going to the spelling match at the schoolhouse tonight, Abe?"

"Of course I'm going, Dennis. I'll be ready in two minutes."

"Oh, yes," said Dennis, but his voice sounded queer. Abe thought Dennis looked queer, too.

"Why did you ask me that, Dennis? You know I always go to spelling matches."

"There's no use for you to go tonight, Abe. They won't let you spell."

"Won't let me spell! Who won't let me spell?"

"The schoolmaster. I saw him this morning. He told me to tell you not to come."

147

"I haven't missed a word all winter," said Abe. "The side I'm on always wins."

"That is just what he said, Abe. He said it wasn't a match when you came—the other side didn't need to try."

That pleased Abe. "I know the spelling book forward and backward," he said.

"You're the best speller on Pigeon Creek," said Dennis. "Everyone knows that."

That pleased Abe, too. "Well," he said, "I'll go, but I'll just sit and listen."

"I guess that will be all right," said Dennis.

The two boys went through the woods to the schoolhouse. They found it full of people— mothers, fathers, uncles, aunts, girls and boys. Everyone was talking and laughing. The people loved these spelling matches, and they would come from miles around. They would come through dark forests. They would cross deep creeks. Neither rain nor snow could keep them at home. They came early, too, so they could visit with one another.

Abe and Dennis were late. They were hanging up their hats when the schoolmaster rang a bell. At once there was silence.

The schoolmaster stood on a low platform. "Jenny Springer!" he called.

Jenny stood up.

"Jenny," he said, "you have the first choice tonight. Begin."

"Abe Lincoln!" called out Jenny.

"No," said the schoolmaster. "Abe can't spell tonight. It isn't a match when he spells. His side is sure to win. Please choose someone else, Jenny."

Now Jenny was a good girl, but she couldn't understand many things. She didn't know whether the world was round or flat. She thought there was a man in the moon. She thought a pound of sugar weighed more than a pound of feathers. So of course Jenny couldn't understand why Abe shouldn't spell.

"I want Abe!" she cried. "I won't choose anyone else!"

"No! No!" cried some voices.

"Abe! Abe!" cried other voices.

The schoolmaster rang his bell. Again there was silence.

Abe stood up. "Jenny," he said, "you must choose someone else. I shall obey the schoolmaster."

Jenny knew that Abe always obeyed the schoolmaster, so she chose someone else.

"Thank you, Abe," whispered the master. "Now sit down and enjoy yourself."

And Abe did enjoy himself. He knew how to spell every word that was missed. When Dennis tried to spell *afraid*, Abe couldn't keep from laughing.

"A-*f-e-a-r-e-d*," spelled Dennis.

"No," said the master, "the word is *afraid*."

"There isn't any such word in my speller," said Dennis. "It's *afeared*."

"Ha, ha, ha!" laughed Abe.

After the match was over the two boys started home. There was no moon and it was very dark in the woods.

"Dennis," said Abe, "are you *afeared?*"

"No," said Dennis, "I'm not even *afraid*."

They both laughed and went through the dark woods whistling.

Johnny Appleseed

It was late in the afternoon when Matilda Johnston came out of the Lincoln cabin and started toward the cornfield. Just then Abe and John Johnston came out of the woods, and Matilda ran to meet them.

"I came after you," she said. "I thought you were here. I knew you'd like to know."

"Know what?" asked John and Abe.

"Somebody's come," said Matilda, "and he's going to stay for supper. Guess who?"

"The preacher," Abe guessed.

"No," said Matilda.

"The schoolmaster," John guessed.

"No," said Matilda.

"I can't guess," said John.

"Neither can I," said Abe.

"It's Johnny Appleseed!" said Matilda.

"Johnny Appleseed!" said Abe. "I've always wanted to see him."

"So have I," said John. "I've heard that he's a queer person."

"He looks mighty strange to me," said Matilda. "He has his appleseeds."

They went into the cabin. There sat the queerest looking man they had seen in all their lives.

He wore a coffee sack with holes cut in it for his arms. He was barefooted. His hair was long —to his shoulders. At his feet were two large bags filled with appleseeds.

He smiled at the boys and asked them if they could lift his bags. John tried, but he couldn't lift either one. Then Abe tried and lifted both.

The stranger was surprised. "Well! Well!"

he said. "I didn't think anybody else could lift my bags."

"They are heavy," said Abe. "Have you carried them far?"

"Five hundred miles," Johnny said.

"Just think of that!" said Mrs. Lincoln. "Five hundred miles through the forest with two heavy bags on your back."

"And then you give your seeds away," said Mr. Lincoln.

"Yes, I give them away," said Johnny. "I want to help people, and this is my way of doing it. There are only a few apple trees in this part of the country."

"And they grew from the seeds you brought here," said Mrs. Lincoln.

"I'd like to see an apple orchard near every cabin," Johnny answered. "It would make the settlers love their homes better. Besides, apple trees will bring more settlers here."

154

"That's true," said Mr. Lincoln.

"What do you do when you are out of seeds?" Abe asked.

"I go back for more," said Johnny, "to the cider mills across the mountain."

"To Pennsylvania?" John asked.

"That's another five hundred miles," said Abe.

"It doesn't matter," said the strange man. "I'm always coming and going."

"Aren't you afraid of Indians?" asked Matilda.

"They have never harmed me."

"But there are snakes in the forest," said Matilda. "Aren't you afraid of them?"

The man looked at his bare feet. "They are tough as leather," he said. "I could stick a pin in them and never feel it. I could step on thorns and never know it."

"But there are the cold and the heat and the storms," said Mr. Lincoln.

156

"I fear nothing," said Johnny, "nothing in the world. I trust the Lord to protect me."

Supper was now ready, and they all sat down at the long table. The visitor thanked the Lord for the food they were about to eat.

The meat was passed to him first, but he refused it. "The children must be helped first," he said.

"There is plenty for them," said Mrs. Lincoln. "They can wait a minute."

"I must see the food on their plates," said Johnny. "I never eat until I know what the children have."

Mr. Lincoln helped the children. Then the visitor took the meat and ate.

After supper Mr. Lincoln said he wanted to buy some appleseeds.

"You may have all the seeds you want, but not one cent will you pay," said Johnny.

"I would rather pay," said Mr. Lincoln.

"You have already paid me," said Johnny. "You have given me a good supper." Then he arose to go.

"You must stay all night," said Mrs. Lincoln.

"No, no!" cried Johnny. "I must be on my way, thank you."

"Where will you sleep?" Mr. Lincoln asked.

"On the ground," said the strange man, "and thank the Lord that I can."

He gave Mr. Lincoln some appleseeds. He thanked Mrs. Lincoln for the good supper. He told them all good-by and went out into the dark forest, alone and unafraid.

"I wish I could do something for people, too," said Abe.

"Maybe you will someday, Abe," said his mother.

How Neighbors Helped

A NEW settler had come to Pigeon Creek with his family—his wife and two young children. They camped out near the Lincolns'.

The stranger began at once to make a clearing. After that he got logs ready for his cabin. But he couldn't lift them and put them in place. No one man could do that.

This stranger had no money to pay helpers. How then could he ever hope to have a cabin?

There was only one way; he hoped the old settlers would help him.

And he did not hope in vain. The word was passed along that the newcomer was ready.

The news went up and down the creek. The miller told his customers. They told their neighbors, and they, in turn, told their neighbors. It wasn't long until everyone had heard the news.

It was good news, too. It gave the settlers a chance to visit with one another all day, for they always took their dinners.

At last the day came. Large baskets were packed with food. Everyone put on clean clothing. The men and boys wore their best coonskin caps and moccasins. The women and girls wore their best dresses and sunbonnets.

From far and near they came—some riding horseback, some in big wagons, some, like the Lincolns, walking.

Then the cabin was begun. The men worked hard, and the boys helped when they could. They couldn't do much because they couldn't move the logs. Abe was the only boy who could work along with the men.

He helped the preacher with a log. Then he helped the schoolmaster and the miller. When he saw little Mr. Bigger puffing and panting, he helped him. When he saw big Mr. Little panting and puffing, he helped him. Abe was here, there and everywhere.

By noon the cabin was as high as Abe's head.

The women had been busy with the dinner. It was spread on long red tablecloths on the ground, and everyone sat on the ground to eat.

There were roast venison, turkey and duck. There were pigeonpie and stewed pumpkin and honey. There were wild strawberries and apples from the seeds Johnny Appleseed had planted. There was maple sugar in gourds, and there were piles and piles of corncakes.

Everyone ate and ate, and everyone talked and talked.

The preacher told a joke which made everyone laugh. The schoolmaster told a joke, too, and everyone laughed again. Mr. Lincoln told an Indian story. Abe told two funny stories which he made up himself.

After dinner the men and boys rested for a while. Then the work began again. Log after log was lifted and put in place. Again Abe was here, there and everywhere.

Before sunset the cabin was finished. The new settler took his furniture from his big wagon and put it in the new cabin.

He thanked the old settlers again and again. His wife thanked them, and they both thanked the women for the good dinner.

Then everyone started home—some on horseback, some in big wagons, some walking through the woods.

Dennis Hanks, Sarah and Abe Lincoln, John, Matilda and Sarah Johnston walked with other girls and boys—all talking, laughing, singing.

Mr. and Mrs. Lincoln left them and went ahead.

"I'm proud of the way Abe worked," said Mr. Lincoln. "Everyone wanted his help."

"Everyone likes Abe," said Mrs. Lincoln.

"They like him because he is so strong," said Mr. Lincoln.

"That isn't the only reason, Thomas. They like Abe, also, because he is smart and good-natured and polite. He will always have friends and good friends, too."

Moving to Illinois

Mrs. Sarah Lincoln stood alone in the little cabin in the Pigeon Creek Settlement. The room was empty. The bureau, chairs and stools were gone. The featherbeds, quilts and spinning wheel were gone. Mr. Lincoln's guns were gone. There wasn't even a coonskin cap on a peg.

Mrs. Lincoln looked about the empty room and began to cry. Just then Thomas came in. "Come, Sarah," he said, "the wagon is loaded and we are ready to start."

"I don't want to go," she said. "We've lived here a long time, and I love our neighbors. I don't want to leave them."

"But I can't make a living here," said Thomas. "I thought this land was good, but it isn't. I can't raise a good crop of anything."

"I know, but I hate to leave Indiana," said Sarah.

"We'll get rich in Illinois, Sarah. They say everything over there grows twice as fast and twice as large. So we'll have all the money we want, and you shall have a new Sunday dress."

Sarah smiled and dried her eyes. Then she followed Thomas outside. There stood the big wagon drawn by four oxen. It was loaded with furniture, featherbeds, quilts, skins, clothing, tools, shovels, saws and many other things. There was even a plow.

There was scarcely room for Mrs. Lincoln, but she climbed up and sat on the load. Matilda and Sarah Johnston walked by the wagon. They were large and strong and could walk miles and miles without getting tired.

Pretty Sarah Lincoln wasn't with them. She had died two years before.

John Johnston, Dennis Hanks and Abe Lincoln were young men now, but they went with the family and walked with Mr. Lincoln.

At night they camped in the woods. After supper they all sat around the campfire and told stories. Mr. Lincoln told Indian stories. He always knew a new one. Abe told funny stories. He always knew a new one, too.

John, Dennis and Abe took turns watching the fire. This time Abe didn't burn all the wood in one big blaze. He kept a small fire burning, but no green eyes came nearer and nearer.

One day they crossed a small river. It was cold weather, and the river was full of chunks of floating ice.

When they reached the other side, they heard a dog barking. And there across the river—on the shore they had just left—was their own dog.

They called him, but the dog was afraid to swim. He was afraid of the floating ice. He ran up and down the shore, barking pitifully. He was trying to say, "Don't leave me here alone! There is no one here to take care of me. I shall starve to death."

"Just listen to him," said Abe. "I can't stand it. I'm going back after him."

"No, Abe," said his father. "We haven't time. We must go on."

"I'll catch up with you," said Abe.

Into the icy river he plunged and swam to the other shore. The dog was wild with joy. He licked Abe's hands, he jumped, he pranced, he barked joyfully.

Then into the icy river Abe plunged again. He held the dog up out of the water and swam with one arm. It was hard work, but he reached the other shore safely.

The wagon had gone, but Abe overtook it. He put the dog in the wagon and walked on with the men.

"He is tenderhearted," said Mrs. Lincoln. "No one else would have crossed that icy river to get a dog."

"Abe couldn't let the dog starve to death," said Matilda. "The others didn't even think of that."

168

"That is what makes Abe different," said her mother. "He thinks of everything."

IN THE NEW STATE

The Lincoln family now lived in a new state, Illinois. Mr. Thomas Lincoln had bought land on the Sangamon River and had built a cabin on the bank of the river.

Abe had helped to clear land for the cabin and a field. He had helped to build the log cabin and fence in the field.

Then Abe left home. He was now twenty-one years old, and he wanted to make a living for himself.

"You have been a great help to me, Abe," said his father. "You have given me every cent you ever earned. I wish I could help you now, but I can't."

"I'm sorry to see you go, Abe," said his step-

169

mother. "You have been very good to me. You have never given me a cross word, and you have never disobeyed me. I love you as if you were my own son."

"You have been good to me, Mother," said Abe. "I will never forget you, and I will help you as long as I live."

Abe carried his clothes in a small bundle. This he tied to a stick which he carried over his shoulder. He had a little money, about twenty-five cents.

He found plenty of work on farms near by. He plowed, chopped down trees and split rails. He husked corn, took care of horses, cows and pigs. He did every kind of work that was done on a farm.

If there was no farm work to be done, he would help the farmer's wife. He carried water, dug potatoes, fed the chickens and churned.

He even took care of the children. He didn't

mind rocking a baby to sleep, because it gave him a chance to read. He rocked the cradle with his foot.

So Abe worked and worked. From sunrise to sunset he worked. But he was never too tired to tell funny stories and jokes. He was never too tired to be kind to everyone.

Before long Abe had many friends. They invited him to Sunday dinner; they told him to stop in when he was passing by. They liked Abe because he wasn't rough and quarrelsome. Most of all, they liked him because he was kind.

One cold day Abe saw a man chopping wood. The man was barefooted and his clothing was old and thin. He was shivering with the cold, and he looked unable to work at all.

Abe felt very sorry for this poor man.

"How are you this cold day?" he asked.

"I'm just about ill," said the man, "but I have to chop this wood. I need shoes."

"Give me that ax," said Abe. "You go home and sit by the fire."

The man thanked Abe and went home at once.

Then Abe swung the ax. And there were few who could swing an ax as Abe could. He knew just how high to lift it. He knew just how hard to strike.

So it wasn't long until the great pile of wood was chopped. It wasn't long, either, until the poor man sold it and bought shoes.

And he was devoted to Abe Lincoln as long as he lived.

Helping the
Helpless

"MOLLY," said the cooper to his wife, "Abe Lincoln has a new suit of clothes."

"Well! Well!" said Molly. "I'm glad to hear that. If ever anyone in this world deserves a new suit, it's that young man."

"That's exactly what I think," said the cooper.

"But how did he ever get enough money to buy a suit?" asked Molly.

"He split rails, Molly. Each yard of the material cost him one week of hard work."

"He must have split hundreds of rails," said Molly.

"He must have," said the cooper. "But it was

173

time he bought a good suit. People were making fun of his clothes."

"Who was?" Molly asked sharply. She liked Abe very much, and she didn't want anyone to make fun of him.

"Oh, the folks who don't want Abe to succeed," the cooper said.

"Of course," said Molly. "They are jealous of Abe because he can make better speeches than any of them."

"Indeed he can," said the cooper. "Abe Lincoln is the best speaker in this state. He is going to speak at the Big Meeting next week."

"I hope he will wear his new suit," said Molly.

"He will. That's why he bought it. He told me so himself."

"Well, no one need be ashamed of Abe Lincoln in his old clothes," said Molly.

A week later, Mr. Lincoln was on his way to the Big Meeting. He was wearing his new suit, and he was proud of it. "No one can make fun of me today," he said to himself. "I look as well as anyone else now."

He was riding horseback on a muddy road, and he rode carefully. He didn't want his new clothes splashed with mud.

Just then he heard a pig squeal. He looked around. There in a field, in a great mudhole, was a little pig.

It was struggling to get out of the mud, but it couldn't. It looked straight into Abe's eyes and squealed again.

Abe said, "I am very sorry, little pig, but I can't help you. This is my new suit, and the mud would ruin it. I hope someone else will get you out."

Then Abe rode on. But he couldn't forget that pitiful squeal. He couldn't forget the fear in the little pig's eyes.

Suddenly he turned his horse and rode back.

He pulled the pig out of the mud and put him
on dry land.

That was fine for the little pig. But it was hard
on Mr. Lincoln's new suit—the suit he had
worked so hard to get—the first good suit he had
ever owned.

Mr. Lincoln arrived at the Big Meeting with
mud-spattered clothes. He was late. The people

had been waiting for him a long time. They were shouting for him now. "Abe! Abe!" they shouted. "Speech! Speech!"

Mr. Lincoln brushed his clothes, but the mud stains showed plainly.

He couldn't keep the people waiting any longer, so he went on the platform and began his speech.

In two minutes everyone forgot the muddy clothes. Mr. Abe Lincoln was speaking! Nothing else mattered.

THE LITTLE TRUNK

Several years passed. Abe Lincoln still lived in Illinois, but he didn't live in a cabin in the woods. He lived in a two-story house in a big town, Springfield.

No longer did Abe plow, chop down trees and split rails. He didn't work on a farm now. He was a lawyer. He had an office in that big town, and everyone respected him and called him *Mr. Lincoln.*

That is what study and good books had done for Abe.

He still worked hard, but it was the kind of work he loved. He worked with books, and he was helping people.

He would ride horseback many miles to get someone out of trouble. He would ride on muddy roads, through rain, sleet and snow.

He still studied at night and sometimes till midnight and past midnight. The more he learned, the more he wanted to learn. He never thought he knew enough.

But he never forgot to tell funny stories and jokes, and he never forgot to be kind. He would go out of his way and neglect his own business to help others. Years later, people still remembered how kind he had been.

"Mr. Lincoln helped me once," said an old lady to three little girls.

"Mr. Lincoln! The great Abraham Lincoln?" asked Helen.

"Yes, my dear," said the old lady. "The great Abraham Lincoln. It was when I was a little girl. I lived in the same town, Springfield, and he often passed my home."

"Did he speak to you?" asked Elsie.

"Always, Elsie. He never forgot to look for me. Mr. Lincoln loved children." Grandma smiled as she remembered.

"How did he help you?" asked Helen.

"I'll tell you the whole story, girls. I was going to visit my grandmother in another city. I had to go on the train and I had to go alone. My father and mother were too busy to go with me.

"But they helped me get ready. Mother made some pretty dresses for me. Father bought a little trunk."

"A trunk!" said the three girls all together.

"Yes, indeed," said the old lady, "and it wasn't a toy trunk, either. It was large enough to hold six dresses, two pairs of shoes, my Sunday hat, a sunbonnet and many other things."

"Did you have a special Sunday dress?" asked Mary.

"Yes, my dear, I did. It was pink, and I had pink slippers and pink stockings. My Sunday hat was pink, too."

"I know you looked beautiful, Grandma," said Mary.

Grandma smiled again as she remembered something else. "I had a pretty pink parasol, too," she said.

"Did you put it in your trunk?" Elsie asked.

Grandmother nodded. "It was the last thing Mother put in," she said. "Then she locked the trunk and Father carried it downstairs. He left it on the porch and went for the expressman.

"I was all ready, so I just sat down and waited. I waited and waited. I talked with Mother. Then I waited some more, but the expressman didn't come.

"It was almost time for the train, so I went out to the gate to look for him. I looked up the street. I looked down the street. Then I looked up and down, and down and up. There wasn't a sign of him!"

"Oh! Oh!" said the girls.

"Then," said Grandmother, "I heard the train whistle, and I knew it would soon be at the station."

"Oh! Oh!" said the girls again.

"What did you do, Grandma?" asked Elsie.

"I cried, Elsie. I cried out loud, too. I knew I couldn't get to the train now.

"Suddenly a tall man crossed the street. He had black hair, gray eyes, and a kind face."

"Mr. Lincoln!" cried the girls.

"Yes, girls, it was Mr. Lincoln. He said he heard me crying across the street and wanted to know what was the matter.

"I told him about my trunk.

" 'Is it a large trunk?' he asked.

" 'No, it's a small trunk,' I said. 'It's there, on the porch.'

" 'I'll take it to the station,' he said. Then he ran to the porch, lifted the trunk to his shoulder and away he hurried to the station.

"I had to run to keep up with him, but I did keep up, and we reached the station just in time.

"The train was ready to go. The conductor was calling, 'All aboard!'

"'Wait for this young lady!' called Mr. Lincoln.

"The conductor helped me up the steps. Mr. Lincoln put my trunk in the baggage car. Then the train began to move.

"Mr. Lincoln waved his hat to me and I waved my hand to him. 'He's the kindest man in the world,' I said to myself. And I have said it ever since, girls. He was always the kindest man in the world."

President of the United States

It was November, 1860. Bells rang! Whistles blew! People shouted! Men hugged each other and threw their hats into the air.

"Abe Lincoln has been elected!" they cried. "Abe Lincoln will be our new President!"

Abe was proud that he had been chosen to become President of the United States, but he was humble, too. He knew that there was much hard work ahead of him. He was used to working hard, and he was determined to do the best job he possibly could as President.

Mrs. Lincoln and the Lincoln boys, Robert, Willie and Tad, were proud and pleased, too.

They were eager to move to Washington. They had several months to get ready, because Mr. Lincoln would not become President until early in March of the next year.

On February 11, 1861, a special train left Springfield for Washington. The Lincoln family and other important people were on the train.

Traveling in a special train was an exciting experience for the boys. All along the way

crowds gathered to watch the train go by. Whenever the train stopped at a city or town, more crowds gathered. At most of these places, Mr. Lincoln made a short speech.

Between stops, he planned what he would say at other cities. Before he left Springfield, he had written a special speech that he was going to give in Washington. He carried a copy of the speech with him in a carpetbag.

The Washington speech was the most important of all the speeches that he was to make. He wanted it to be just right. When he had a little time on the train, he would get the speech out of the carpetbag and go over it again.

One afternoon when he was working on this speech, Willie and Tad became very restless and noisy. At last Mrs. Lincoln said, "Boys, I wish you would be more quiet. Your father is trying to finish his Washington speech."

Willie sat down beside his mother at once.

"Do you mean the speech he will make at his inauguration?" He said the long word carefully.

Ever since Mr. Lincoln had explained that he would not be President until after his inauguration, Willie and Tad had tried to use the word. They thought that it had a fine sound.

"Yes," Mrs. Lincoln nodded, "that's the one. Many people are waiting to hear what your father will say in that speech."

Mr. Lincoln stopped working on his speech and put it back in the carpetbag.

"Well, well," he said. "Is anybody ready to do a little wrestling?"

"I am! I am!" Willie and Tad shouted.

"Oh, Abe," Mrs. Lincoln said. "You're tired. Besides, you have so much to do."

Mr. Lincoln chuckled as he wrestled playfully with the boys. "I'm never too tired or too busy to spend time with my sons."

And he never was. No matter what problems he faced, no matter how busy or tired or worried he was, he found time for his boys.

By the time Abraham Lincoln went to Washington, some of the Southern states had withdrawn from the United States of America. The people in these states had set up a country of their own, the Confederates States of America.

The Northern states were called the Union. Mr. Lincoln did not believe that the United States should be divided into two countries. The people in the Union agreed with him. The people in the Confederate States did not agree. About six weeks after Lincoln's inauguration, the War between the States began.

President Lincoln hated the cruel war, but he believed liberty and union were worth fighting for. He believed the North and South should be one nation.

He also believed that all the people were important in any government. In one of his speeches he said that "government of the people, by the people, for the people, shall not perish from the earth."

Abraham Lincoln worked long hours, day and night, during the war. There was no end to the problems that he had to solve. Through it all, he found time to help many people.

Every day soldiers came to see him. Widows and mothers of soldiers came, too. He always did everything he could for them.

Mr. Lincoln felt sorry for all the people who were hurt in the war. He felt sorry for their families. Even in these sad times he went on telling jokes and stories. He tried to make people laugh. He knew it was important to keep cheerful and to be good-natured.

In the fall of 1864, Abe Lincoln was elected President again. The war was still going on, but now it looked as if the Union would win.

A few months later President Lincoln made

his second inauguration speech. He asked the people of the North and the South to forget their bitter feelings. He wanted them to work together to "bind up the nation's wounds."

In April, 1865, the war finally ended. Once more the flag of the United States was raised in the South as well as in the North.

Mr. Lincoln was happy that the war was over. He was glad that the Union had been kept. He knew that there were still many problems ahead, but he was sure that they could be worked out. Above all, he wanted all the people in all parts of the country to be treated fairly.

One day soon after the war ended, Mrs. Lincoln insisted that her husband go for a drive into the country with her.

"You are tired, Abe," she said. "A drive will rest you, and the countryside is beautiful at this time of year."

The President left the papers on his desk and

went to the carriage. Together, he and his wife drove into the country. Abe laughed happily as he watched a robin fly into a tree with a long string in her bill.

"She's building a nest, Mary," he said. "And we will build a new nation. The North and the South will be one nation, truly united."

Mary Todd Lincoln smiled at her husband. She was thinking of the long road he had traveled from the backwoods to the White House.

The little boy who had lived in a little log cabin in a little clearing on a little creek had become one of the greatest men that the world has ever known.